Happy New Year!

I hope 2007 is going to be a great New Year for you. It certainly is going to be an exciting year for Harlequin Romance! We'll be bringing you:

More of what you love!

From February, six Harlequin Romances will be hitting the shelves every month. You'll find stories from your favorite authors, as well as some exciting new names, too!

A new date for your diary...

From February, you will find your Harlequin Romance books on sale from the **middle of the month.** (Instead of the beginning of the month.)

Most important, Harlequin Romance will continue to offer the kinds of stories you love—and more! From royalty to ranchers, bumps to babies, big cities to exotic desert kingdoms, these are emotional and uplifting stories, from the heart, for the heart!

So make a date with Harlequin Romance— in the middle of each month—and we promise it will be the most romantic date you'll make!

Happy reading!

Kimberley Young
Senior Editor

"What's this?"

Rick handed a package to Anne. "Chopsticks, so you can practice."

"Is there going to be a test later, or something?"

"You never know." The slow words raised gooseflesh on her arms, and that was before he winked.

"You know, you can be surprisingly charming when you put your mind to it," she said. Then she leaned over and kissed him on the lips.

It was a simple expression of gratitude, she told herself.

Which was why she found it absurd when fire shot through her veins with scorching force....

JACKIE BRAUN
The Businessman's Bride

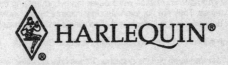

TORONTO • NEW YORK • LONDON
AMSTERDAM • PARIS • SYDNEY • HAMBURG
STOCKHOLM • ATHENS • TOKYO • MILAN • MADRID
PRAGUE • WARSAW • BUDAPEST • AUCKLAND

ISBN-13: 978-0-373-03929-6
ISBN-10:   0-373-03929-8

THE BUSINESSMAN'S BRIDE

First North American Publication 2007.

Copyright © 2006 by Jackie Braun Fridline.

"I've always believed that each person ultimately determines his or her own destiny, but my heroine, Anne Lundy, has her hands full trying to convince Rick Danton that who he is biologically is not as important as who he chooses to become."
—Jackie Braun, *The Businessman's Bride*

* * *

Dear Reader,

Which shape us more—our genes or the choices we make? In *The Businessman's Bride,* Anne and Rick are each sure they know the answer. Anne Lundy, who is adopted, is positive DNA doesn't matter. Rick Danton, who harbors some ugly family secrets, is just as certain it does.

I enjoyed putting their beliefs to the test and exploring the way that love not only heals hearts, but can make families out of strangers.

I hope you enjoy their story, as well.

Best wishes,

Jackie Braun

For Bill, Izumi and Yui.
Many thanks.

CHAPTER ONE

"I NEED you."

Anne Lundy was independent enough that the words scraped her throat coming out, especially since the person she found herself needing was none other than the man whose office she'd stormed out of a month ago, right after telling him to stay the hell out of her private life. Yet, here she was, in that very same room, preparing to ask him to butt back in.

Richard Danton stared at her from the other side of his orderly desk. Not for the first time Anne thought that the polished mahogany surface mirrored his person. There was never so much as a speck of lint on his expensive tailored suits or a hair out of place on his patrician head. God help her, but sometimes as irritating and confounding as she found the man, her fingers itched to muss up those perfectly combed auburn locks and loosen his collar. It might be interesting to get a rise out of someone who was so damned controlled all of the time.

Oh, yes, definitely controlled, she thought now. The only sign that either her words or her unannounced visit had surprised Rick was the slight quirking of his left eyebrow.

"Why don't you have a seat," he invited. He picked up his telephone, pressed a button on the cradle. "Hold my calls, please," he told his executive assistant. Then he focused his attention on Anne. "I believe you were saying something about needing me."

"Is that a variation of 'I told you so'?" she asked between gritted teeth.

"Of course not." He folded his hands in front of him on the desk blotter. "What can I help you with, Miss Lundy?"

Anne wasn't sure why, but she'd always felt Rick used that courtesy title and her last name as a way of distancing himself from her. No matter. Their relationship wasn't social. At times she thought it barely qualified as cordial. If she had to classify it, she supposed it might fall under business since he was employed as chief legal counsel for Tracker Operating Systems, the computer empire that Anne's older brother, J.T., owned and operated.

Rick apparently took her familial association with Tracker as reason enough for him to pry into her personal life. During the past few years he had investigated at least four of the men Anne had dated. In truth, something about the hasty retreat of a couple of her earlier boyfriends also raised suspicions, although Anne had no hard evidence that the private eye Rick kept on retainer for company business had been sicced on either man.

It still galled her to recall how absolutely unapologetic he'd been last month when she'd called him on the carpet for his most recent interference. She'd tromped into his office in high temper, spoiling for a fight. It had only ticked her off more that Rick never so much as raised his voice. The man rarely did.

"Your brother is the CEO and founder of one of the most successful computer companies on the planet. He's a very wealthy and powerful man," he'd told her in that patronizingly patient way of his, as if J.T.'s billionaire status had somehow managed to escape Anne's notice. "That kind of wealth and power can draw…unsavory characters."

Damn him, but she'd known Rick was right about her current beau even before he had proved that to her—with photographs no less.

Even now that her bruised ego had had a month to heal it still rankled that she'd been suckered by Gabe Deerfield's phony interest in her hand-tinted photography when in truth he hadn't been entranced so much by Anne or her art as he'd been eager for an in at Tracker. It turned out the jerk was a software architect for one of J.T.'s smaller competitors.

"I want you to look into a personal matter for me," she told Rick now, swallowing a little more of her pride when both of his eyebrows notched up.

"A *personal* matter?" he repeated, acting as if he hadn't heard her right.

Anne scowled. "Yes. A *personal* matter."

"That's interesting, Miss Lundy, because the last time you were here you said—"

"I know what I said," she interrupted. "And I meant it. I *still* mean it. I don't appreciate you poking around in my private life, Rick, even if my big brother does. But…" She cleared her throat and admitted, "I need help and I can't go to J.T., or anyone else in my family, on this. Not yet anyway."

That statement had Rick straightening in his high-backed leather chair. The bored amusement had vanished from his expression by the time he asked, "What is it?"

Just like that, she had his undivided attention. As irritating as the man could be at times, Anne knew this was something she could count on. Rick always listened to what she said—even if he didn't often heed her wishes.

She settled onto one of the chairs angled in front of his desk and crossed her legs. Her foot jiggled and one of her spiked heels dangled from her toes, exposing her nerves.

"It's probably nothing, but a couple weeks ago I got a call from a man who claims to have information about my birth mother. You knew I was adopted, right?"

She smiled afterward, since she figured that much was obvious. With her Asian features and diminutive height she was the polar opposite of the rest of the tall, blond-haired and blue-eyed Lundy clan.

Rick nodded solemnly. "J.T. mentioned it to me, but I was under the impression that your biological parents were both…well, deceased."

"They are." She shrugged then, swallowed. "I mean, that's what I've always been told, which is why I hung up on the guy the first couple of times he called. Whatever this information is, assuming he even has any, it's ancient history as far as I'm concerned."

"How many times have you spoken to him exactly?"

"Only a few times." She coughed. "But he's left a few or, um, eleven messages on my answering machine."

Rick steepled his fingers in front of him and frowned. Anne knew what he was thinking. Sure enough, he said, "And you're just now bringing this matter to my attention, Miss Lundy? He could be a stalker."

She fought the urge to roll her eyes. "You're determined to make me regret coming here today, aren't you?"

Rick said nothing for a moment. Controlled, she thought again as she watched a muscle twitch briefly in his jaw.

"So, what does he say when he calls?" he asked at last. "Does he ask for payment in exchange for the information or in any way hint that he knows you are related to J.T.?"

"No. He's never mentioned money and J.T.'s name has never come up."

Anne fiddled with the clasp on one of the bracelets looped around her left wrist. In truth, that was one of the things about the situation that bugged her. The man wouldn't tell Anne the nature of his information, but he didn't seem to be threatening her with it. Nor had he named a price to reveal it. If he had, she would have figured his claims were part of some creative scheme to bilk money from her brother.

She looked up at Rick then. "Has J.T. mentioned anyone approaching him with a similar claim?"

It would be just like her overprotective big brother to keep something like that to himself until he could verify the man's story independently.

But Rick said, "No. I've heard of nothing."

It went without saying that if there was anything to hear, Rick would have heard it. J.T. trusted no one's insight or advice more than he trusted Rick's. Anne relaxed slightly. The last thing her brother needed right now, with his wife heading into her third trimester of pregnancy with their first child, was to be chasing down some crackpot's claims.

"Of course, that doesn't mean the guy won't show up at Tracker with his palm out," Rick added.

"I suppose."

"But?"

"It's just that the man keeps insisting on a meeting, saying that what he needs to tell me isn't something he wishes to share over the telephone."

Anne motioned with her hands, unable to keep them still any longer. When she talked, she tended to use her entire body. The beads from her bracelets tinkled together. The sound was cheerful, festive and in direct contrast to her troubled mood. "It's making me a little edgy, like I'm waiting for the other shoe to drop."

"A minute ago you said whatever he had to say was ancient history," Rick reminded her.

"It is, but he's been so persistent. Polite, but...persistent." She cleared her throat. "It's kind of creepy, if you know what I mean."

"I'll look into the matter."

She smiled. "Thanks."

"You've got a name or some other contact information for me, I assume?" he asked.

Anne dug a piece of paper out of her oversize bag and handed it to him. After reading it, Rick glanced up sharply.

"Gidayu Hamaguchi? That's a Japanese name."

"Which is handy since he claims to be an attorney from Japan," Anne remarked dryly.

Rick's expression remained thoughtful. "Isn't that where you were born, Miss Lundy?"

She knew what he was getting at. Her origins weren't exactly common knowledge. In fact, most people who didn't know the particulars of her personal history probably assumed Anne was of Chinese or Korean descent, since cross-cultural adoptions from those two countries had been relatively common for years and were much less restricted than those from Japan.

"He could have gotten lucky," she said hopefully.

Rick's expression said he wasn't buying it. He pulled a yellow legal pad from his desk drawer and picked up his fountain pen. "Why don't you tell me what you know about your biological family?"

Anne stood and prowled the length of the room. As a general rule, she wasn't one to sit still for long. That was especially the case when her nerves were jangling the way they were at the moment.

"Well, I know that my mother was a Japanese college student and my father was an American serviceman stationed in that country. I think they were married and they both died, although I'm not sure how or exactly when. After that I somehow wound up placed for adoption in the United States."

"You don't know anything else?"

"That's actually a lot more than most adoptees were told nearly three decades ago," she pointed out. "Oh, and I know they called me Ayano, which is still my legal name, by the way."

"Ayano. Ayano Lundy," he repeated. His voice took on a surprisingly lyrical quality as he tested out the syllables. "It's pretty and it suits you."

She shrugged. "I prefer Anne."

"Of course."

While he made some notes, she studied the collection of framed photographs on the equally tidy credenza. As far as she could tell, none of the people pictured with Rick was family. Judging from the sterile settings, conservative attire and stiff poses, she determined all of them to be business associates—which was kind of sad, in her estimation.

Then she came to the last photograph and recognized the subjects instantly. J.T. stood with his arm looped around the shoulders of his bride, Marnie, next to whom was Anne, laughing merrily. She remembered the moment—her brother's wedding the summer before. She just didn't remember Rick capturing it. The candid photograph seemed oddly sentimental amid the rest of the stodgy shots that were framed atop the credenza.

Anne picked it up and turned toward Rick. "Where'd you get this?" she asked.

He shrugged, looking curiously uncomfortable for

a long moment before stating the obvious: "I took it at your brother's wedding."

She studied it again.

"Hmm, subject matter is good even if your technique needs a little work. Lighting's not too hot and J.T. has a serious case of red-eye." She glanced up, grinned. "Of course, I think I saw him crying when he and Marnie exchanged vows, so maybe that's not you or your camera's fault."

He ignored her attempt at humor and tapped his pen on the pad of paper. "Can we get back to the matter at hand, Miss Lundy?"

"Sure." Gazing again at the picture, she felt the comforting swell of love for her family. "You know," she murmured, "I never really think of myself as adopted. I just think of myself as a Lundy."

"But you must have questions," Rick said. "You must want to know…details about your real parents."

"My *real* parents?" Anne set the frame aside and, after turning, crossed her arms over her chest. Her tone was sharp when she asked, "What makes those other people more real than Jeanne and Ike Lundy?"

"I'm sorry if my choice of words offended you." But then he dug himself in deeper when he said, "I just mean that, biologically speaking, they're responsible for the person you are, who you've become."

"You can't believe that, Rick. You can't believe that who I am, other than physically, was somehow predetermined by my DNA?" When he said nothing, Anne waved a hand, "Well, I don't buy it, but now isn't the time to debate free will or nature versus nurture. The fact remains that my birth parents have been dead for nearly twenty-nine years. I guess that has always made it easier for me to move on."

"And yet you still want to know what information this Japanese lawyer has on your mother."

"Birth mother," she corrected automatically. "And my curiosity doesn't extend beyond wanting to know if this Hamaguchi character is an actual attorney or if he is some kind of criminal out to fleece Tracker. If he's the latter, I'll press charges. If he's not..." She shrugged. "Well, then he can say his piece and get out of my hair. It's not like there's anything he can tell me after all this time that will change my life."

Anne believed that wholeheartedly. She'd long ago accepted that the how and why of her becoming a Lundy were irrelevant. She had a secure foundation, a loving family in Ike and Jeanne and J.T. Indeed, she no longer cared that anyone who met her brother or her parents knew right away that she wasn't related biologically to them. Once upon a time that had bothered her. Once upon a time, she'd had questions. No longer. She had no doubt that the bond she shared with her adoptive family was every bit as unbreakable as one rooted in blood.

"Very well. I'll look into it right away and call you when I know something."

Anne retrieved her purse and looped the wide strap over her shoulder. Rick was being so decent about the whole matter that the way she'd treated him during their last meeting in his office weighed heavily on her. As much as she hated to admit it, some sort of apology was in order.

"Look, Rick, about the last time I was here… I said some pretty nasty things to you and called you some vile names."

"Vile names?" That single eyebrow rose. "I don't remember any vile names."

"Oh." She coughed to cover her embarrassment. "I guess I didn't call you those directly to your face. I'm afraid I have a bit of a temper."

"*You,* Miss Lundy?"

"I'm trying to apologize here," she reminded him pointedly.

He made a circular motion with the pen. "Well, by all means, proceed."

His lips curved then and Anne realized that even though Richard Danton didn't smile often or with a wide show of teeth, the effect still managed to turn his pleasant features into something strikingly handsome. Why had she never noticed that before?

"A-a-anyway," she stuttered momentarily before regrouping. "I know that at the time I told you I didn't need another big brother. I mean, J.T. is a large enough pain in my butt given the way he insists on holding up the magnifying glass to my personal life all of the time."

"An apology," Rick reminded her.

"Um, yes. Well, then this matter came up and…" She shrugged. "I guess what I'm saying is that maybe it's not so bad to have you acting like my big brother—well, just every now and then."

Rick was no longer smiling.

"Apology accepted," he said tightly, and it dawned

on Anne that she hadn't really said she was sorry. Was that why he suddenly looked so irritated?

"Thank you for doing this," she told him again.

He nodded. "No problem, Miss Lundy. I'm more than happy to act in your brother's stead."

He didn't look "more than happy," though. But before she could remark on it, he was motioning toward the door.

"I'll call you when I know something. Now, not to be rude, but I have some work I need to get back to."

"Oh, sure. Sorry." She tucked her hands into the back pockets of her jeans and edged awkwardly toward the door. "See you around."

The second the door to his office closed behind Anne, Rick launched his fountain pen across the room. It ricocheted off the credenza with enough force to snap the pricey writing implement in two. But that wasn't what had him cursing so lavishly.

"Big brother." He spat out the words, muttering a few creative expletives as he yanked at his tie and then raked a hand through his hair in utter frustration.

Though he'd always been careful to hide it, Rick had been attracted to Anne since J.T. had introduced them six years earlier.

He still recalled every detail of that day clearly, right down to what Anne had been wearing: white poet's blouse, snug-fitting blue jeans and a pair of sexy high heels that had added a few inches of height to her otherwise petite frame. She'd walked into her brother's office to a tinkle of beads from the half-dozen bracelets looped around her slim wrists, the corners of her eyes had crinkled with a smile, and Rick had felt the world slip away beneath his feet. She was that gorgeous.

Then she had opened her mouth and begun speaking and he'd been by turns entranced and amused. In addition to being beautiful, the woman was witty, smart, interesting, original, a little irreverent and a lot likable.

Six years later, Rick still thought so, which was why he had been careful to maintain his distance. Apparently he'd done a good job if she thought of him as a surrogate sibling.

"I don't want to be your damned big brother, Anne," he muttered before slumping back in his chair.

Yet he knew that a more serious relationship with her—his boss's baby sister of all people—just wasn't in the cards. For that matter, a serious relationship with any woman wasn't.

Not for someone with a pedigree like Rick's.

He didn't allow himself to wallow in self-pity. He didn't believe in it. He believed in action, hard work and staying so busy that he didn't have time to dwell on things that couldn't be changed, and his family history was definitely one of those things. So, within minutes of Anne's departure, he had tidied his appearance, secured a new fountain pen and was dialing the number from the slip of paper she'd left with him.

It was for a hotel not far from Fisherman's Wharf. From the name of the chain that the woman at the front desk gave upon answering the telephone, Rick knew the accommodations were moderately priced, but a couple weeks worth of lodging still added up. The cost would set the Japanese attorney—or whoever he was representing—back a good chunk of change. That bothered Rick. What sort of information was worth such an expense?

He asked for Gidayu Hamaguchi's room and his call was put through. Even though it was midafternoon, a man answered on the first ring, almost as if he'd been sitting next to the telephone, eagerly awaiting contact.

"Gidayu Hamaguchi?" Rick asked.

"Yes. I am Hamaguchi."

"My name is Richard Danton. I'm calling on behalf of Anne Lundy."

Rick was pretty sure he heard the other man sigh in relief. He wasn't quite sure how to interpret that.

"I am pleased to speak with you, Mr. Danton. I hope Miss Lundy is well?"

"Miss Lundy is fine, other than wondering why you keep calling her."

"I am sorry if my telephone messages have been disturbing to her, but I did not wish to arrive at her home without first securing an invitation."

The man knew where Anne lived? That fact had Rick's blood running cold and so his tone was clipped when he said, "Let's cut to the chase."

"Cut to the chase?" Gidayu repeated slowly. Then comprehension apparently dawned. "Ah, yes. Cut to the chase. You have questions you would like answered, yes?"

Gidayu's pronunciation held enough of an accent that Rick could tell English was not his first language, even though he was obviously fluent. His fluency revealed something about the man's character, as far as

Rick was concerned, since he knew it took dedication and hours of study to get to that level. Rick decided to reveal a little something about his own character.

In flawless Japanese he replied, "I have only one question. You have contacted Miss Lundy on several occasions claiming to have information about her birth mother. What is the nature of that information?"

There was a brief pause. "Your Japanese is very good, Mr. Danton."

"So is your English."

And Gidayu switched back to it when he said, "As I have told Miss Lundy, it is not something I wish to discuss over the telephone. It is a sensitive matter."

"Who sent you? Who do you work for?" Rick demanded in Japanese.

"More questions?" Gidayu's tone held humor. "Unfortunately I am not at liberty to say at the moment."

Rick nearly smiled at the mini-power struggle that was playing out in two languages, but the reference to this being a sensitive matter and Gidayu's overall secrecy quelled any humor.

"When can you meet?"

"I will make myself available whenever Miss Lundy has the time," Gidayu said.

"Miss Lundy will not be coming to our meeting. I will meet with you and pass on the information about her birth mother—if and when I deem it to be authentic," Rick stressed. "And I wouldn't suggest you try contacting her again, either by telephone or in person."

He was sure he heard a sigh this time, and he had little doubt that its origins were not rooted in relief.

"Very well," Gidayu said at last.

By the time Rick hung up, he and Gidayu had agreed on a meeting time and place for the following afternoon. Rick sipped his coffee, which had grown cold, and walked to the credenza. Glancing down at the photograph of Anne, he exhaled slowly. Soon enough, she would have the answers she sought. Rick just hoped that whatever it was Gidayu was so determined to share about her birth mother was something Anne ultimately would appreciate knowing.

In his experience, some family secrets were best never revealed.

CHAPTER TWO

SINCE her first successful gallery show a couple of years earlier, Anne had leased the upstairs rooms of a Victorian on Greenwich Street between Baker and Broderick in San Francisco's Cow Hollow neighborhood.

She couldn't quite swing the rent on what she earned for her hand-painted photography, even though her career was coming along nicely. At her most recent show at Javier's, for instance, an anonymous collector had paid handsomely for an exclusive collection of scenes focusing on lovers that Anne had shot in a small park near the waterfront. Even so, her income fluctuated dramatically from month to month. She could only afford the apartment because her brother helped foot the bill.

She'd balked at first and in truth she still wasn't entirely comfortable with the arrangement. She preferred to earn her own way. But she loved San Francisco, not to mention the view of the bay that was visible from her living room windows. On days when the fog burned off, she could see Alcatraz Island, and if she leaned over the sill and squinted hard, she could just make out the Golden Gate Bridge.

That vista helped ratchet up the rent in what was already an expensive city. So she had accepted J.T.'s help, knowing full well that the apartment was a compromise. After all, he'd made it clear that he would prefer to see her living in some gated community with armed guards and attack dogs standing at the ready. Her big brother worried about her.

And maybe for good reason, Anne thought as she settled into her seat in the spare bedroom that she had converted into a studio.

Just over a week had passed since she'd choked down her pride and gone to see Rick. As efficient as the man was, he'd already met with Gidayu Hamaguchi and was now in the process of determining if the Japanese lawyer really was who he said he was and if his claims were legitimate. What exactly those claims were, Anne didn't have a clue because Rick wouldn't say. Indeed, he wouldn't offer so much as a hint. He wanted to ensure that every "i" was dotted and every "t" crossed first, he told her. Such thoroughness might be admirable under other circumstances, but in this case it was taking a toll on Anne's nerves.

She nibbled off another bite from the chocolate bar that was doing double duty as her breakfast and her lunch, and picked up her paintbrush, determined to lose herself in work. That wasn't so hard, really. Anne loved her job, which she'd always thought of as more of a calling than a career. Art, after all, beckoned. Its lure was as seductive as a siren's summons, even though it never made any promises to pay the bills.

Some people, Anne supposed, might wonder why

she didn't just shoot the same subject matter in color film rather than black and white, and be done with it. But to her way of thinking each careful stroke of her brush to the matte finish added more than color. It imbued emotion, energy. Done right, the oils she chose embellished and enhanced real life, creating an alluring alternative reality. Best of all, the process married Anne's two greatest loves: photography and painting.

The telephone rang just before her brush touched the photo's surface. Even as she cursed the intrusion, she was swiveling in her chair so that she could reach the cordless handset. The caller ID readout listed an unfamiliar cell number. She debated letting the machine pick up the call, but then decided to answer and give whoever was on the other end of the line a blistering earful. She was in that kind of mood.

"This better be good," she warned in lieu of a greeting.

She had to shout the words since she liked to listen to music when she worked. The stereo was on and tuned to a jazz station that was playing a tribute to Coleman Hawkins. The volume was high enough that certain notes had the glass in the windows vibrating. Turning it down would be a simple matter, not to mention the courteous thing to do, but Anne didn't plan to carry on a long conversation, let alone a polite one.

"Having a bad day, Miss Lundy?" a familiar deep voice asked. He didn't need to say, "This is Rick Danton." But he did so anyway.

"Rick." The identity of the messenger and his possible message had her heart kicking out an extra beat. She reached for the remote and switched off the stereo. "Sorry. I don't like to be disturbed while I'm working."

"I never would have guessed," he drawled. "By the way, was that Coleman Hawkins?"

Anne felt her mouth drop open and it was a full ten seconds before she recovered the power of speech. "You know Coleman Hawkins?"

"The Father of the Jazz Saxophone," he confirmed.

As a teenager, Anne had gone through a rap phase that had sent her Motown-loving brother into raging fits. She smiled now, since that had been half the fun of listening to The Beastie Boys. Her subsequent fondness for pop had been met with no more enthusiasm. Now, just the other side of thirty, she had developed a taste for jazz. J.T. remained as baffled by her musical metamorphosis as he was unimpressed with her latest preference in genre. Some people, she knew, just didn't get jazz. How was it possible that Rick was one of the people who did?

"You like jazz?" she asked, just to be sure.

"What's not to like?"

Exactly. Still, his taste in music seemed utterly incongruous with his person. It was hard to picture someone as seemingly controlled and by-the-book as Rick Danton embracing freewheeling improvisation. Anne couldn't help wondering: Had she missed something?

To cover her consternation, she teased, "Maybe there's hope for you yet, Danton."

She heard him clear his throat. "Yes, well, as fascinating as I find this conversation, music is not the reason for my call."

"No. I didn't figure it was." Anne stood and paced to the window. It was raining outside and had been all morning. It was a constant drizzle that made her wish the sky would just open and get it over with already so the air could clear and the sun could shine. She took a deep breath, anxious for her own personal downpour to begin. "So, what have you found out?"

"I'd prefer to deliver my findings in person."

Anne closed her eyes and groaned. "Come on, Rick, just spill it already. All this cloak-and-dagger business isn't making me feel any better."

"Five minutes, Miss Lundy."

"Five minutes? Wh-what…you're coming here? Now?"

The thought had her panicking. Friday was cleaning day and this was Thursday, which meant her apartment was barely habitable let alone fit to receive company. Glancing down, Anne realized that neither was she, since she'd planned to spend the day holed up in her studio rather than out in public with her camera.

Working at home could be both a blessing and a curse. There was no need to struggle into panty hose and power suits or balance a bagel on one hand while navigating traffic during the morning commute. That was the blessing. The curse was just this scenario: an unexpected visitor when Anne was still wearing the same wrinkled cotton drawstring pants and camisole she'd slept in. She hadn't bothered to apply any makeup, although she had run a brush through her hair at one point.

"I'll meet you somewhere," she offered, hoping she

didn't sound as desperate as she felt. She glanced at the half-eaten candy bar and inspiration struck. "Have you had lunch?"

"No, but—"

"Good. There's an Italian restaurant a couple of blocks over. They make the best manicotti in the city. It'll be my treat."

"Not necessary, really. Your apartment's on Greenwich, right?" And then he rattled off her address. "I'm almost there."

"Fine, but drive really slow, Danton," she ordered just before hanging up.

Anne rushed to the living room and shoveled the accumulation of clothes, magazines and junk mail off the couch, dumping it in the small closet just off the entryway. As she struggled to close the door behind the deluge, she knew if Rick wore an overcoat, she wouldn't be offering to hang it up.

If she wanted to dress and slap on some eyeliner, she wouldn't have time to tidy the kitchen. So she tossed a dish towel over the small mountain of plates, bowls and pans heaped in the sink, and called it good. Not for the first time she regretted that room was separated from the apartment's main living space by a mere half wall.

As she tugged on a pair of slim-fitting jeans and a long-sleeved red T-shirt, she glanced at the clock. Five minutes had stretched into ten, as she'd hoped they would, since finding a place to park in her neighborhood wasn't easy. Plus, it was raining out, making those spaces that much more precious. If her luck held, she would have another five minutes to do something with her hair and face.

Anne had managed a ponytail and was applying some lip gloss when the buzzer announced Rick's arrival. Satisfied that both she and her apartment looked presentable, she went to the intercom and pressed the button that unlocked the door downstairs.

Rick hadn't even cleared the first landing before he was admonishing, "You should have asked who it was before letting me in."

Anne was tempted to close her apartment door in his face. "Why would I ask? I knew it was you."

"How?" he challenged, that solitary eyebrow arching as he approached.

"Let's just say I'm telepathic," she replied through gritted teeth.

"Oh, you're something all right, Miss Lundy."

He'd reached the top step and, given his height, she was forced to look up at him. His hair was damp, she realized, and, while still tamed to its usual tidiness, the humidity seemed to have pushed it to the verge of curling. That beguiling half smile she remembered made an appearance and some of Anne's anger was diffused.

"Come in," she said.

As she'd feared, he wore a trench coat over his usual impeccable suit. He shrugged out of it and glanced toward the closet, but Anne took it from his hands and, offering a thin smile, laid it atop a tall stack of newspapers that were destined for recycling.

"Why don't we have a seat?" she invited, steering

Rick toward the couch, which faced away from the kitchen. But he didn't sit. Instead he walked to the bay window and glanced out.

"I bet on a clear day you have a great view of the water," he remarked.

"Yes." When he turned back toward her, she gestured meaningfully toward the couch, but he started toward the hallway on the far side of the room instead and Anne had the sinking feeling she'd forgotten to close her bedroom door. She hadn't made her bed that morning, but that wasn't the worst of the room's deficiencies, she knew. She tended to let clothes and other things accumulate on the floor before making a massive sweep to restore order. That massive sweep hadn't occurred yet.

"I considered renting an apartment in this neighborhood when I first moved to San Francisco," he was saying conversationally.

"Oh? Where did you move here from?" she asked, hoping that if she stayed in the living room as she spoke, so would he.

He hovered at the opening of the hallway, his gaze straying down it. "Pennsylvania. I went to college there." Then, "You know, I've always wondered what the inside of these homes looked like. They look so incredible from the street."

"Well, I'd love to give you the grand tour," Anne told him. "But the place is a little messy. I gave my cleaning lady the day off."

"Really? Never would have guessed." He faced her and one side of his mouth lifted briefly. Then, seemingly apropos of nothing, he asked, "Might red be your favorite color, Miss Lundy?"

She glanced down briefly at her shirt, which was deep crimson, but when she looked back at Rick in question, he had turned and was once again staring down the hallway.

Anne came up behind him and followed the line of his vision. Her bedroom door was indeed open and the place was as disheveled as she remembered, but that wasn't what had her face heating. No, it was the sight of her pajamas lying in a heap on the floor where she'd stepped out of them just a few minutes earlier. And right next to them was a pair of high-cut red silk panties.

She brushed past him and pulled the door shut with a smart click.

"I wasn't expecting company," she reminded him pointedly.

Rick nodded and she figured he'd taken her not so subtle hint to get back to business, but then he walked farther down the hallway, bypassing the bathroom. He paused at the last door, which also was open. "So, this is your studio?"

"Yes, but I don't like—" Unbelievably he strolled into it. "People poking around in there," she told his back.

With a strangled sigh, Anne followed him. She planned to shoo him out, but then she realized that the room was probably the tidiest one in her apartment. She preferred order when she worked and had long ago designated her studio as a clutter-free zone.

Tucking her hands into the back pockets of her jeans,

she watched Rick prowl every inch of the small space. He appeared genuinely fascinated by the assortment of paints and brushes set up on the table near her work station. Then, he moved to the wall where Anne had hung some of her most recent works. She liked to see them framed and matted. It gave her an idea of how they would look hanging on the gallery walls at her next show.

Even though Rick had picked through her personal life on Tracker's behalf on several occasions, his nosiness now came as somewhat of a shock. It was almost as if he were driven to answer some deep-seated questions.

She cleared her throat noisily, drawing his attention. He at least had the grace to flush.

"Sorry." Then he waved a hand back toward the wall. "Do you mind?"

Anne opened her mouth, intending to tell him yes, but she found herself shaking her head instead and asking, "So, what do you think?"

"They're good. All of them, but this one is..."

He tapped the frame of a scene from a local street festival. It was busy, its action so fluid that it had an almost sensual quality. Anne had used vibrant colors to capture and convey all of the energy and verve. She considered it one of her most inspired works. It came as a surprise to realize she was holding her breath as she waited to hear his opinion.

"It's exceptional," he said at last.

"It's my favorite," she confessed on a smile.

"You have an incredible knack for picking just the

right colors and then using them to draw attention to the smallest of details."

It was something Anne had been told before. Indeed, the art critic for the *Chronicle* had written as much in his review of her last gallery show. But coming from Rick, the assessment seemed to carry more weight. Perhaps because Anne sometimes felt he didn't see her as anything more than his boss's flighty younger sister.

"Thank you," she said.

"You're welcome." He pointed toward the tilted surface of her desk. "Mind if I take a peek at what you're working on now?" he asked.

Normally Anne didn't like anyone to see her work before it was finished, but she found herself nodding. Somehow she doubted he would be put off by her refusal anyway. Rick Danton had never struck her as the sort of man who took no for an answer.

"A portrait this time." His eyebrows shot up as he studied the black-and-white photograph of Jeanne Lundy, which Anne had just begun to imbue with ethereal hues.

"Why do you seem surprised?"

"I'm not. I mean, from what J.T. has said, I guess I just didn't think you did portraits."

She joined him at the desk and admitted, "Well, it is a bit of a departure for me. Generally speaking, other than the inherent motion in street scenes, I prefer inanimate objects such as building facades or other man-made structures for my subject matter."

"Like your Golden Gate Bridge series."

The hand-tinted photographs to which he referred had earned Anne critical acclaim and the numbered prints continued to bring in a tidy sum. Still, she frowned.

"I wasn't aware you were familiar with my work," she told him.

"J.T. has a couple of those prints in the conference room at Tracker."

"Oh. Of course." It was a simple and yet oddly disappointing explanation.

Then he surprised her once again by saying, "But you've used people as subject matter before."

"For my lovers series, yes. But those focused on clasped hands, linked arms, that sort of thing. Not faces," she said slowly.

"So, what made you decide to branch out into portraits?"

Rick settled onto the low ledge of the room's large window as he spoke and braced his hands on each side of his hips. The pose made him seem younger, more relaxed, and Anne found his open curiosity about her work engaging.

"I don't know. I was thinking this might make a nice gift for my mom. Her birthday is coming up."

"I'm sure she'll like it."

Anne shrugged, and maybe because Rick seemed so genuinely interested and so approachable for once, she admitted to him what she had told no one else. "I've found doing portraits difficult and because of that, well, exciting."

"Your own personal Everest?"

She nodded, pleased that he understood what she had only recently begun to suspect.

"Faces have so many..." She gestured with her hands as she searched for the right word.

"Dimensions?"

"Yes. The moods they can reflect are so varied, so complex. Obvious ones like joy and anger, but I'm finding capturing the more subtle ones to be the real challenge."

"Subtle ones?"

Something flickered in his expression. There and gone as quickly as a spark from a campfire.

"Loneliness or need, maybe even longing," she murmured, searching his features.

"It sounds like you're talking about the kinds of emotions people try to hide."

"Or control." What had possessed her to say that?

"It does sound challenging. After all, you never really know what someone else is thinking, what they're feeling."

His fingers drummed softly on the windowsill—a show of nerves or impatience? His expression remained bland, though. Anne blinked and smiled awkwardly. Surely she'd been mistaken.

"Maybe not," she agreed. "Maybe all the guesswork involved is why faces intrigue me."

That was especially true of the face of the man before her, she realized. Since that day in his office when Anne had watched the way a sardonic half smile could so transform his features, her curiosity had been piqued.

It was the curiosity of an artist, not that of a woman, she told herself. After all, his eyes were such an interesting blend of gray and green that it would take great skill and patience to replicate, let alone enhance, the color with her oils. And then there was his mouth, which was wide, the top lip just a little fuller than most men's. Depending on the colors she chose she could make it appear pliant or demanding.

"You'd make a good subject, Rick."

"Hardly," he scoffed. The fingers stopped drumming and the mouth she'd been staring at flattened into a taut line.

"No. I mean it." Anne closed the short distance between them, too intrigued by his features to question the wisdom of her actions as she stepped into the gap between his legs. Since Rick was sitting on the windowsill, the two of them were nearly eye level, which made it easy for her to frame his face between her hands. "You have great bone structure."

His cheeks were warm against her palms—hot almost. The contact, benign as it was, seemed to transfer a good deal of that heat to Anne, driving up her own body's temperature. The moment stretched insanely before Rick's fingers covered hers. She swore he pressed her palms tighter against his face for just a moment before he pulled her hands away. Then he straightened and Anne was forced to step back.

"I think we should get down to the reason for my visit, Miss Lundy," he said stiffly.

Where a few minutes ago he had seemed more than happy to put off discussing his findings, now he sounded almost impatient to begin.

"Good idea." Anne's heart bumped unsteadily

against her ribs, the origins of her nerves not completely clear. To lighten the mood, she quipped, "I feel like there should be a drumroll or something, you know?"

Rick's expression, however, remained grim as he reached into the breast pocket of his suit coat and extracted a thick white envelope.

"First of all, I suppose I should tell you that Gidayu Hamaguchi checks out. He is just what he claims to be, an attorney from Japan."

"And you're sure he's not after money or out to hurt or embarrass J.T. in some way?"

"I don't believe so. He has information about your adoption that he wants to share with you. Information that, as far as I've been able to determine in so short a period of time, appears authentic." He tapped the envelope meaningfully. "He's representing…a client in Sapporo."

"Okay, so what's his big news concerning my birth mother that he wouldn't discuss over the telephone?" She took a deep breath and exhaled slowly. "Was she some kind of criminal or a hooker or a drug addict or something?"

Anne had had a lot of time for her imagination to work up various unsavory scenarios. Even if the truth turned out to be more disturbing, she figured she could deal with it, as removed as she was from the situation. After all, what had gone on nearly thirty years earlier didn't have any bearing on her life now. It didn't have anything to do with who she had become.

"It's nothing like that," Rick replied, but after that

reassuring bit of news his next statement detonated like a bomb. "She's alive, Anne."

"What?" It took a moment for his words to register, partly because for the first time she'd known him, Rick had used her given name. "Who's alive?"

"Your birth mother."

CHAPTER THREE

"MY BIRTH mother is alive?"

The question came out a little on the high-pitched side, so Anne took a deep breath, exhaled slowly and tried again with, "Are you sure?"

"Well, she claims to be your birth mother and certain things check out. Her name is Chisato Nakanishi."

"I don't want to know her name!"

The vehemence in Anne's tone surprised them both. Knowing the woman's name made her too real. Of course, Anne knew she was being ridiculous. The woman *was* real. She was real, she was alive and she had made contact.

"I'm sorry, Rick. Go on. Please."

His expression remained sober and something about the intense way in which he was regarding Anne made her think she hadn't heard the worst of it.

"Why don't you sit down?" He motioned toward the chair near her desk.

His suggestion did nothing to quell her nerves. Anne shook her head. She damn well would stand for this news, whatever it was.

"I'm fine." She crossed her arms over her chest and tilted up her chin. "Just spit out the rest of it already."

"Very well." He cleared his throat. "Chisato Naka-nishi claims that she never consented to your adoption. According to her, she and your father divorced—"

"The *baby's* father," Anne interrupted stubbornly. "We still don't know that her baby was me."

"The birth dates match and your first names are the same." But Rick nodded. "You're right, we don't know for certain and I think, given your brother's wealth, it's imperative we establish her identity beyond a shadow of a doubt before things progress too far."

She liked the official sound of that. It allowed her some distance. Anne's tone was more normal when she said, "So this couple divorced?"

"Yes, when the child was still a baby. The father took the baby without Chisato's permission to the United States."

"He was American?" Her heart skipped a beat.

"Yes. His name was Roger Hastings and he was a member of the U.S. military stationed at an air base near Tokyo. That's where he and Chisato met. She was—"

"A college student."

When Rick nodded Anne swore her heart started to pound out "Taps." This more fleshed-out version of events fit so seamlessly with the skeletal one she had long known.

"Hastings was killed in a car accident just outside Boston," Rick was saying.

Holding onto the tattered remnants of her skepticism, she said, "Okay, assuming I was this baby, how did I wind up placed for adoption?"

"Chisato's not exactly sure," he admitted. "But Gidayu Hamaguchi said they believe Hastings's parents may have arranged it through a friend of theirs. The man was an attorney. He was under suspicion for baby trafficking before he died of a heart attack seven years ago. No charges were ever filed and the case kind of fizzled after his death. Not enough evidence."

Anne shook her head vehemently. "Baby trafficking. The Lundys —"

"Would have had no reason to suspect anything," he assured her. "Neither Gidayu nor Chisato are making any accusations in that regard."

Still, Anne remained uneasy, queasy.

"But why would the Hastingses do that?" What Rick was saying seemed utterly incomprehensible, especially since the people in question might very well be her paternal grandparents. "Why wouldn't they just send… the child back to her mother after their son's death?"

Rick couldn't quite meet her gaze. "The Hastingses were an old money family from the East Coast. In addition to money, they had standing in their community and power. Their son was a bit of a rebel. He had enlisted in the service instead of following his father into the family business, that sort of thing. He was their only son and they had high expectations. When he married Chisato, they didn't approve." He cleared his throat. "Apparently they had hoped he would settle down with a woman from their…social circle."

Anne snorted indelicately, anger charging well ahead of her other emotions. "There's no need for political correctness, Rick. It wasn't the social circle they had a problem with. It was the fact that she was Japanese."

He said nothing, but then he didn't need to. Anne had run into that kind of small-minded bigotry on more than a couple of occasions growing up. Even her brother's vast wealth didn't insulate her from it now that she was an adult.

"I'm sorry," he said quietly.

"No need for you to be." She was silent for a moment, then: "You said Roger and Chisato were divorced."

"Yes."

"But a divorce wasn't good enough for his parents," she said knowingly. "Not when he'd already produced an heir. Even their son's death wouldn't have changed the fact that if the baby remained with Chisato, it would remain a Hastings. That's what they found so disturbing, I'll bet."

"Perhaps," he said slowly, but he didn't appear to be disputing her assertions.

"So, they had one of their cronies help them arrange an adoption. Out of sight, out of mind."

"That's what Chisato believes." Rick's tone carried a hint of sympathy when he added, "I'm afraid some people can't accept differences."

Anne glanced at the desktop. The black and white image of Jeanne Lundy smiled back at her and it helped wipe away some of the bitterness. "And some people can. Some people celebrate differences."

Rick nodded. "Getting back to Chisato, she didn't have the money or resources to fight back."

"So, she gave up," she said sadly.

Whether or not Anne was that baby, she found it impossible not to feel sorry for a woman who had been denied the right to raise her own child because of someone else's pettiness and intolerance.

"No. Chisato never gave up. She's been searching ever since."

Anne swallowed hard. That wasn't what she had expected him to say. It wasn't, she realized, what she had *wanted* him to say. It had been easier to think of the other woman moving on with her life before somehow stumbling onto a lead a couple dozen years later.

"It's been nearly three decades. She's been looking for…her child all this time?"

"Apparently."

Anne closed her eyes. "God, all this time," she said again, her voice a hoarse whisper.

"I haven't been able to verify the information completely," Rick stressed. "And, as you said, we don't know for certain that you were the baby."

But Anne was only half listening. Damning phrases from their conversation now played back through her head, whirling with centrifugal force.

Chisato never consented…

Taken without her permission…

Searching ever since…

Anne hadn't searched. Indeed, she had put this part of her life to rest a long time ago, and with full burial honors no less. Yet here it was being exhumed. No, not exhumed, resurrected. In her heart, she knew, her birth mother had just come back from the dead.

The blood began to rush and roar in her ears, making

it difficult to hear, but she thought she heard Rick say, "A DNA test would be the best way to determine the truth of her claims."

"Blood." Anne felt queasy, light-headed.

"Actually I think they'd just need an oral swab."

It didn't make her feel any better that no needles would be involved.

"Miss Lundy?"

"I think I will sit down," she said, trying for nonchalance and failing miserably when she stumbled backward and groped for the chair, which skittered across the hardwood floor on its casters.

Rick was at her side in an instant, guiding her toward the seat. As the room tilted and her heart squeezed, he knelt in front of her, pressed one of his big, warm hands onto the back of her neck and forced her head between her knees.

She should have been mortified. At the moment, though, she could only muster slight embarrassment and an appalling amount of gratitude as he massaged her nape with surprising gentleness and instructed, "Breathe. Come on, Anne. In and out. In and out. That's it."

It took a few minutes, but the worst of her dizziness finally passed.

"I don't need this now," she mumbled as she gazed at her feet.

The sentiment was utterly selfish, but she meant it.

She was a grown woman—happy, well-adjusted and coming into her own professionally. Okay, her love life stunk, but even that wasn't overly troubling to her. She'd always figured that when the right man came along, she would know it and everything would fall into place.

"You're going to be okay," Rick said quietly.

His fingers stroked the sensitive skin just below her hairline. His touch felt good. It felt comforting, although something about that description seemed off just now. Of course, her entire life seemed a little off.

"I didn't ask for this," Anne said.

She was angry suddenly and not quite sure what to do with that anger. All she knew for certain was that she didn't want some blast from her distant past intruding on what appeared to be a promising future. The phrase "searching ever since," however, implied that it would.

As quickly as it had come, though, Anne's anger ebbed. If Chisato Nakanishi was who she claimed to be and if everything had happened the way she claimed it had, then that woman was the biggest victim in this tragedy and, at the very least, she deserved answers.

She also deserved some kind of closure.

Raising her head enough so that they were eye level, Anne told Rick, "It's not fair."

Indeed, if Chisato was right, nothing about the situation was fair to Anne or to either of the two women who claimed Anne as their daughter.

Eyes that were not quite green and not quite gray regarded her solemnly. The fingers that had been massaging her neck trailed away to skim down the length of her ponytail, which had slipped over her shoulder and hung between them. When his fingers reached its end, Rick frowned at his empty hand.

"Life is seldom fair, Miss Lundy."

Anne told herself it was only so she could avoid thinking about the upheaval in her personal life that she pointed out, "Do you realize that a minute ago you called me Anne, and now I'm back to being Miss Lundy? Why is that?"

Rick blinked and his mouth worked soundlessly for a moment. The man who seemed to have all of the answers all of the time was suddenly at a loss for words.

"Well?" she prodded, amused. Amazed.

Rick reached out and she thought he might caress her cheek, but his hand bypassed her face entirely and settled on her crown. He wasn't quite so gentle when he ducked her head between her knees this time.

"Just breathe," he ordered brusquely before rising to his feet.

Rick tried to follow his own advice, but there didn't seem to be enough oxygen in her small studio. He paced to the window, unlocked it and cursed himself for a fool as he cranked open the glass. The damp June air cooled his skin, but he still felt as though he were on fire. Hell, he'd felt ready to combust since arriving.

He should have agreed to Anne's suggestion to meet at a restaurant. Then he could have told her what he'd discovered with a few feet of linen-covered Formica separating them. Better still, he should have gone straight to J.T. and let her brother deliver the news. But no, Rick had not only honored her wishes to keep this information from the man who signed his paychecks, he'd come to her apartment to discuss it with her in person. Once here, of course, he'd been compelled to look around and satisfy his curiosity. He'd found himself almost desperate to know if, during those weak moments when forbidden thoughts of Anne managed to slip past defenses, his imagination was right about the place in which he pictured her living and working.

A minute ago you called me Anne, and now I'm back to being Miss Lundy. Why is that?

Because I remembered who I am, he thought grimly.

Oh, he'd forgotten for a while there, especially right after she'd touched him. When her small hands had bracketed his face it was more than physical distance that had been breached. Rick's control had very nearly snapped like a wishbone. For one insane moment he'd considered kissing her. That had been the case again just now when he'd knelt before her, his fingers stroking her soft skin.

Thank God he'd come to his senses both times.

It wasn't only what he assumed J.T.'s reaction would be that had held him in check. He simply had no right. Not with Anne or any woman.

He knew that, just as he accepted that no amount of education or polish or passage of time could purge the ugliness from his past. Nor could it eradicate the damning reality of heredity.

He glanced down at his hands. They were so like his father's with their wide palms and long, tapered fingers. They were the kind of hands a concert pianist would envy. They were hands capable of extreme violence.

Taking a deep breath, Rick extricated himself from the memories. It wasn't the secrets of his past that had brought him to Anne's apartment. It was the secrets from hers.

She was sitting up when he turned. Her forearms were braced on her thighs, her hands clasped loosely between her knees. And she was watching him. Her face was still pale, her lips slightly pinched. He saw questions in her dark, almond-shaped eyes and he had the uneasy feeling that not all of them were about Chisato Nakanishi.

He chose to ignore them.

"Better?" he asked blandly.

"As well as can be expected under the circumstances, I suppose."

"So, you're not going to pass out on me?" He raised one eyebrow, knowing how the gesture nettled her.

Sure enough, irritation replaced wariness. She rolled her eyes and sighed. "That was just low blood sugar, Rick," she snapped. She motioned toward the remains of a candy bar perched on the corner of her desk. "I haven't had much to eat today. I guess it made me a little light-headed."

"The news was pretty upsetting, too."

She said nothing.

"Maybe we should leave the rest of this for another time," he suggested.

"No. I'm fine. Go on."

She waved a hand and he realized she wasn't wearing her usual assortment of jewelry. Typically her every movement seemed choreographed to the music of tinkling beads. Sometimes, the sound could help him gauge her mood, but he couldn't quite figure it out now. He'd just turned her world upside down, although she appeared to be rallying. It was one of the things he admired about Anne. She never stayed down for long.

He stooped to retrieve the envelope from the hardwood floor where he'd dropped it when he'd helped her into the chair. It had shaved about a dozen years off his life when he'd watched her turn so unnaturally pale and then wobble backward.

"Gidayu made copies of the relevant legal documents—records of Chisato and Roger Hastings's marriage and divorce and the birth of their daughter. They're in Japanese, but from what I can tell they appear authentic."

"You can read Japanese?"

"One of my many talents. I'll leave them with you."

He handed the envelope to Anne, but she made no move to open it.

"What now?" she asked.

"That's your call."

"Does she want to meet me?"

"Yes, but a DNA test should be conducted first," he stressed again.

Anne nodded, but she didn't say anything for a full minute. Instead she swiveled in the chair so that she sat in profile to him, facing the desk. As he watched, she took one slim finger and traced the curve of Jeanne Lundy's cheek in the photograph.

"I guess I figured as much," she said at last. "I mean, if I were in her shoes and I thought I'd finally found my long-lost daughter, a reunion would be my goal."

"I think you need to talk to your parents and J.T.

They'll want to know and they can offer you better advice than what I can."

She turned and smiled then. "Oh, I don't know. You've done pretty well. I don't think J.T. could have done any better."

If she made a comment about his acting as her big brother, Rick figured he'd have to punch something. But she was saying, "You're right about a DNA test, though, even if part of me is already pretty sure about what it will reveal."

"I'll contact Gidayu and make the arrangements."

Anne stood. "Thank you, Rick."

"You're welcome." Silence stretched awkwardly. "Well, I should be going and let you get back to work."

"Something tells me I won't be getting much done this afternoon," she replied wryly. "I'd hoped to finish this portrait today or at least get a good start on it since my mother's birthday is coming up, but I'm not in the right mood to do it justice now."

"What are you in the mood for?" The query just slipped out.

Anne's eyebrows shot up. "That's an interesting question. You know, coming from a different man, I might take it the wrong way," she teased.

"If I were a different man I might mean it the wrong way," Rick told her. He wasn't joking. One side of his mouth crooked up, though, to mitigate his words, and he added, "I guess it's a good thing that I'm just Rick."

She made a little humming sound in the back of her throat that had his molars snapping together.

"Well, Just Rick, want to play hooky with me?"

The tempting offer tugged at him, but he knew he should get back to the office. He had a meeting scheduled at three and a stack of paperwork that needed his attention before then.

Even so, he heard himself say, "Maybe. What do you have in mind?

"Why don't we start with lunch? I really should eat."

"Okay." He'd planned to grab something on the way back to the office anyway. He mentally reshuffled his schedule. Some of the paperwork could wait. "On the telephone earlier you mentioned something about an Italian restaurant being nearby. Manicotti sounds good."

Anne tilted her head sideways. "I don't suppose you know a good sushi bar?"

"You're kidding, right?"

"No."

"You live in San Francisco, Miss Lundy. This city is home to some of the finest Japanese cuisine outside Asia."

She wrinkled her nose. "Sushi is made with raw fish. I've never had a taste for it."

"Raw fish," he scoffed. "That's actually sashimi. Sushi is really more about the rice and the way it's prepared. Even so, you don't know what you've been missing."

"Why don't you educate me then?"

Rick swore the smile that wreathed her face had his heart stopping. And that was before she added, "And why don't you call me Anne?"

CHAPTER FOUR

Rick drove to a Japanese restaurant that wasn't far from Anne's apartment. Its storefront was so nondescript that she had never noticed it before even though she'd passed it on numerous occasions.

"We're eating here?" she asked dubiously.

"Trust me," was all he said.

Of course, the small establishment didn't offer valet parking and the rain was coming down harder by the time he parked his car. His choice in transportation had been another surprise. Rick drove a sporty two-seater that seemed totally at odds with his buttoned-down image. She'd figured him for a conservative sedan, something beige and sedate that would coast along at the posted speed limit. This red foreign number had moving violation all but stamped on its hood, especially with a lead-foot like Rick shifting gears and zipping through the afternoon traffic as if he were trying to qualify for the big race at Daytona.

He offered to drop her off at the door, but Anne wouldn't hear of it.

"I have an umbrella and I'm willing to share."

Rick's hair was still damp from his last dash through the rain. They'd had this same conversation when leaving her apartment and he had declined then, too.

"Not necessary. I'm fine," he said.

He got out of the vehicle and hurried around it to open her door. As independent as Anne considered herself to be, she nonetheless appreciated the gesture. There was something to be said for a man who treated a woman with a little old-fashioned courtesy. She frowned then, realizing that the last three men she'd dated hadn't bothered to hold doors or engage in any of the other little niceties her mother insisted revealed a man's true character.

"If he doesn't treat you well in public, Anne, how will he treat you behind closed doors?" Jeanne Lundy had said on more than one occasion.

Anne had to admit, her mother's assertion had proved accurate too often to be a fluke.

Rick's overcoat was dotted with rain by the time he swung open her car door and waited for Anne to put up the umbrella. She'd ordered the umbrella through her sister-in-law Marnie's mail-order business, charmed by the festive row of silk daisies affixed to its edges. The flowers helped chase away some of the afternoon's gloominess. She doubted they earned points with Rick or any other member of the opposite sex, though.

"Come on. Get under already," she said. "It's pouring."

His gaze strayed to the daisies and that single eyebrow lifted. She decided not to give him a chance to decline this time. Raising her arm, she shielded his head from the worst of the weather. Of course, the move required her to step in and that brought Anne into close proximity with his rock-solid build. God, he was tall. Even wearing the spiky high heels that added a few inches to her diminutive height, the top of her head was still level with his chin. And he smelled good. She remembered that from her studio.

"Your hair's already soaked," she murmured.

"It'll dry."

She surprised them both by reaching up with her free hand to run her fingers through it. She smiled then. "It wants to curl."

Rick cleared his throat. "Which is why I keep it cut short. We'd better get inside."

They hurried to the door in an odd huddle that had their hips bumping intermittently. One of his hands was wrapped around the umbrella's handle, partly covering hers. For some reason, the entire scene struck Anne as intimate, which was ridiculous.

"Watch your step," he said when they reached the door.

Thinking of the strange direction her thoughts had taken, she said, "Maybe I'd better."

"Excuse me?"

"Nothing. It's just that…I'm starved." Smiling brightly, she added, "So, how are the burgers here?"

When he scowled, Anne grinned. "That was a joke, Rick. Honest. I promise to try sushi or sashimi or whatever else you recommend."

"Do you mean you're going to listen to me for a change, Miss Lundy?"

"Not if you call me Miss Lundy. Anne, remember?"

He nodded, exhaling slowly.

After the hostess showed them to their table it

became clear Rick was a regular. The owners even came over, bowing in greeting and then chatting amiably with him in Japanese. He introduced them to Anne and they said something to her.

"Sorry, but I don't speak the language," she apologized in English.

They said something to Rick in Japanese that had him shifting uncomfortably in his seat as his gaze strayed to Anne. He shook his head, muttered something that had the older couple frowning, but then the conversation switched to English.

"Enjoy your meal," the older man told her, before he and his wife retreated.

When they were gone, Anne remarked dryly, "I take it you've been here before."

"A time or two."

"Do you eat out a lot?"

He nodded. "Probably a little too often, but it's convenient, especially when I work late."

Left unsaid was that he did that a lot. She recalled J.T. saying he was always after Rick to knock off early or to take an extended vacation. Her brother had even offered Rick the use of his beachfront home on Mexico's Baja Peninsula, but without success. The man apparently was a workaholic. Interesting, Anne thought now, but she hadn't had to twist his arm very hard to get him to play hooky with her today.

"What about you?" he was asking.

She stared at him blankly, trying to recall what they had been talking about.

"Eating out," he coached after a long pause.

"Oh. Sure. I live on takeout. There's a deli around the corner from my apartment that delivers the best stacked turkey on rye in the bay area. And up the street from that is an Indian restaurant whose chicken curry is to die for."

"Can't cook, huh?"

"I burn toast," she admitted without a shed of embarrassment. "Mixing, measuring, watching a timer…it's just not my thing. What about you?"

"I can manage a simple meal without the fire department showing up on my doorstep, but it's not much fun cooking for one."

Even though it was absolutely none of her business, she found herself wanting to know. "Have you ever been married?"

"No."

"Really." Her gaze took in his square jaw and enigmatic eyes. "Ever been close?"

He shook his head.

"Got the hots for someone right now?" She wiggled her brows, hoping to add a little levity to her not-so-subtle grilling.

He didn't say anything. Instead he picked up his menu.

"Oh, come on, Rick. You know the net worth, eye color and underwear preference of every man I've dated during the past few years. Turnabout is fair play."

Without glancing up, he said succinctly, "I'm not involved with anyone, okay?"

"Okay."

Anne hoisted her own menu and glanced at it for a moment before tipping it down so that she could study his face. She'd meant what she'd said earlier about his great bone structure. She'd love to shoot his portrait and then work on tinting it.

"So, why don't you have a girlfriend?"

"I can recommend the *nigiri* made with either tuna or eel," he said, his gaze never straying from the menu. "If you're up for sea urchin, then their *gunkan* is some of the best in the city."

"You're not going to answer me."

He did glance up then. "No."

"Fine." She shrugged. But she found she couldn't let it go. A moment later she was saying, "It's strange, though. I mean, you're a good-looking guy."

Rick rolled his eyes and turned the menu over to the back page where the beverage selections were listed. Even so, she got the feeling that her assessment of his looks made him uncomfortable based on the way his lips were pressed together.

Anne continued anyway. "You appear to have a nice body under those suits, which you wear very well, by the way." Her gaze slid appreciatively over his broad shoulders. "I'm guessing you work out regularly."

He shifted in his seat. Was he blushing?

"And you're obviously well educated and gainfully employed," she added.

He set aside his plastic-coated menu with an impatient snap. "Don't forget that my teeth are real."

She chuckled. "And here I thought those were caps."

"Miss Lundy—"

"Anne."

"Could we talk about something else?"

Anne rested her elbows on the tabletop and plunked

her chin down in her palms, enjoying herself immensely. She didn't bother to hide her grin when she asked, "It's damned annoying having someone sniffing around in your private life, huh?"

"Not the same in the least," he said with a brisk shake of his head. "After all, I don't attract the same kind of self-centered users you do."

"Ouch."

He sighed, looked contrite. "I'm sorry. That was uncalled for."

"But you meant it."

And, she realized, his bald assessment, while hardly flattering, was nonetheless accurate. Or, at least it had been recently. That should bother her and yet it didn't, because none of those men had really mattered to her. Clearly a bruised ego was much easier to get over than a broken heart.

"Miss Lundy—"

"Anne." She corrected him again and then waved a hand in dismissal. "Let's forget about me and the kind of men I tend to attract. What kind of women do you attract or, better yet, what kind of woman do you think is attractive? Maybe I can help you find a date."

He closed his eyes on a long-suffering sigh. "The waitress will be back in a moment for our orders. Do you know what you want?"

A thought occurred to Anne then. "You're not...I mean, not that there would be anything wrong with... I just wouldn't have guessed... But then this *is* San Francisco."

A muscle ticked in his jaw. "I'm not gay."

"Thank God!" The words came out oddly emphatic. When his eyebrows rose, Anne picked up her own menu and tapped the sashimi selections with her index finger. "So, what was it that you recommended?"

When she'd invited Rick to lunch, she'd figured they would grab a quick meal, maybe talk a little bit more about the particulars of the situation with Chisato and then Anne would return to her apartment and he would be on his way. A couple hours, tops.

Nearly three hours later they were still sitting in the restaurant, Chisato's name had come up only once and Anne was actually enjoying herself.

Rick was surprisingly interesting. Anne prided herself on having an open mind, but she had to admit she'd judged Rick on appearances alone. Based on his conservative attire and reserved demeanor she'd assumed he was dry and boring, the kind of guy who tuned into C-SPAN for entertainment and read legal briefs for enjoyment. It turned out he was a closet Comedy Central watcher as well as a fan of Dave Barry.

He also had an amazingly adventurous palate. Anne had let him talk her into trying half a dozen dishes and she'd found that she liked them all. Well, except for the one made with octopus.

"Texture takes some getting used to," he'd agreed, and then he'd reached across the table to adjust the chopsticks she held in her hand. "Remember, no stabbing. That's considered incredibly poor manners."

He was quite proficient with the things, whereas Anne had wound up with more than a few bites in her lap rather than her mouth.

Just before three o'clock he'd glanced at his watch, frowned and politely excused himself from the table to make a phone call, presumably to reschedule whatever it was she'd taken him away from with her impromptu invitation. Anne appreciated the way he'd stood in the small foyer of the restaurant to make the call rather than gabbing into his cell while seated across from her. That was one of her pet peeves and, truthfully, she'd fully expected Rick to do just that.

In her experience, self-important business types were among the worst offenders of restaurant etiquette. But then today Rick had proven that he wasn't quite the man she'd always assumed he was.

"I have a confession to make," she told him now as she finished off the last of her green tea. "I haven't always liked you."

"Really, Miss Lundy?" Rick's brows shot up dramatically. "That comes as a complete shock."

She was tempted to kick him under the table, and not just for the sarcasm, but because even though she had asked him repeatedly to call her Anne, he insisted on using her last name and adding that damned courtesy title.

"You know, sarcasm is often a defense mechanism."

She said it flippantly, but then wondered if maybe she was on to something. After all, she'd known Rick Danton for the better part of six years and despite their many conversations—or, rather, their many confrontations—he remained an enigma. Today, though, she thought she'd caught a glimpse of the real man and she liked what she saw.

"You're not going to start spouting penny psychol-

ogy at me, are you? If so, I'll get the check." He glanced
at his watch and frowned. "I guess we should be leaving
anyway, unless you want to stay and have dinner."

"I'll pass on both the penny psychology and the
second meal, but I'll get the check." When he opened his
mouth to protest, Anne said, "I insist. It's the least I can
do."

Rick let her pay the bill, but on their way to the exit
he ducked into the kitchen. Through the circular
window in the door, she saw him talking with the wife
of the owner. When he came out a moment later, he was
carrying a small bag.

He handed the package to Anne.

"What's this?"

"Chopsticks," he said. "So you can practice."

She was touched…and a little nervous, given the
gleam in his eye. "Is there going to be a test later or
something?"

Who would have guessed that the thought of
spending more time with Rick would hold such appeal?

"You never know." The slow words raised gooseflesh on her arms and that was before he winked.

It was no longer raining by the time they reached her
street. People were outside, walking, jogging and
enjoying the reprieve in the weather.

"You can just drop me off in front of my apartment,"
Anne told him when he slowed his car to parallel park
in a spot a few houses up the block.

"I'll walk you to your door."

Anne opened her mouth to protest that it wasn't necessary. It wasn't like this was a date or anything. But she decided against it. This *wasn't* a date, but whatever it was, she found herself oddly sorry to see it end.

"You know, my day had its ups and downs, but I had a really good time this afternoon," she said as they ascended the steps to the porch of the Victorian. "You can be surprisingly charming when you put your mind to it."

"Charming." His lips twisted.

"That was meant as a compliment, you know," she said on a laugh.

"Ah. That explains it."

"What?"

"I just don't hear many of those coming from you."

"Keep it up and that will be the last."

"See? Now, that's more like it." He took the key from her hand and inserted it into the lock. Holding open the door, he said, "I'll call you."

At her surprised look, he cleared his throat and clarified: "To let you know what Gidayu Hamaguchi has to say about the DNA tests."

"Oh. Sure. Great." She crossed the threshold and Rick started to leave. He was halfway down the stairs when Anne hurried onto the porch and called his name.

He turned, his right foot rising to rest on the next step up. "Yes?"

Anne wasn't sure what she'd intended to say or why it had seemed so important to stop him from leaving just yet. But there he stood, waiting for her to continue, so she began with the obvious: "Th-thanks again. For everything. And I really appreciated the fact that you shuffled your schedule for me this afternoon."

He nodded and his left foot joined the right one, bringing him one step closer to her.

"Is that all?"

Anne shook her head slowly, descending one step and then two until they were eye level.

"I really… I really want to…"

Thank you. The words, despite being redundant, were what she planned to say, but they ebbed away and evaporated like mist as her gaze dipped to his mouth. Pliant? Demanding? Which would it be? Curiosity begged her to find out. She leaned over and kissed him on the lips she'd found so fascinating when they'd stood in her studio.

It was a simple expression of gratitude, she told herself, even if she did linger a little longer than she would have when, say, kissing her brother. Still, the peck was platonic by every conceivable measure. In Hollywood it would have earned a G-rating. Which is why Anne found it absurd when fire shot through her veins with scorching force.

Shocked, she slid one foot back until her heel thunked against wood. She felt as unsteady as a child who had just learned to walk as she lifted her feet and retreated, stumbling backward, stair after stair, to the porch. Rick didn't move. Nor did he blink. He watched her intently, unreadable emotions churning in his gray-green eyes with all the force of a tropical storm.

From the safety of her porch, Anne smiled and waved briefly, attempting nonchalance. Then she couldn't stop herself. She touched her lips, tracing them lightly with her fingertips. Good Lord, they seemed to tingle.

"Bye," she murmured.

Rick's nod was brisk, although he said nothing before he turned on his heel with the precision of a drill sergeant. The soles of his wing tips slapped rhythmically at the soggy treads on his speedy descent. Just before reaching the sidewalk, though, he stopped and executed another about-face.

His expression was fierce, angry almost as he stood there, breathing deeply. If she were to photograph it and then paint it in oils, she would choose vivid reds and stormy grays and greens.

He didn't say anything and so Anne asked, "Did you forget something?"

"Lost something."

"Oh?"

"My mind," she thought he said.

The response had Anne's heart pounding, her pulse tripping, and that was before Rick started up the stairs, taking them two at a time. He didn't stop when he reached her. He grasped her by the shoulders and his forward momentum carried them both backward until her shoulders connected with the wood of the door. Anne felt its ornate brass handle press into her spine.

His hands touched her face, his fingers weaving into the hair that was pulled back at her temples. In that instant before his head lowered and his mouth found hers, she felt his thumbs stroke her cheeks.

Nothing about this kiss could be labeled platonic, especially when he angled his head to one side and her lips parted. It was an urgent, insistent assault on her senses, and an incredibly erotic one despite the fact that they were standing outside in full view of her neighbors and the passing traffic.

When it ended Anne realized she was clutching the lapels of his overcoat and one of her calves was twined around his. She also was huffing as hard as if she'd just jogged up San Francisco's dizzying Lombard Street. She couldn't catch her breath. She felt shell-shocked. What's more, she felt duped. How could a man who kissed like that have been under her nose all this time? It made her wonder what other skills he possessed and what else might be lurking beneath that tidy, gabardine-clad exterior.

"Wow." That single syllable came out on a gusty sigh.

Rick, she realized, didn't appear to be as dazed as she felt. It was almost as if he had anticipated all of that heat and sexual need. At least he was breathing just as heavily as she was. That soothed her ego some, even though he looked just as angry as he had when he'd charged up the steps toward her.

"I didn't mean for that to happen," he stated flatly and stepped away, extricating his leg from hers and forcing her hands to release their grip on his overcoat.

In spite of his scowling expression and less than flattering assertion, Anne was amused. "Well, I don't think it could be called an accident. Are you going to claim that your lips slipped?"

"Miss—"

Amusement fled. It was her turn to be mad now. "So help me God, Rick, if you don't call me Anne after that, I'm going to have to hurt you."

"I shouldn't have kissed you like that."

"Oh? How should you have kissed me?" Before he could reply, she said, "By the way, on a scale of one to ten, I'd give it a twenty."

Despite her teasing tone, she meant it. She hadn't expected to feel that kind of physical interest in someone she had known and not particularly liked for six years, but then her life lately had definitely been full of the unexpected.

"Look, I was out of line."

"It's okay," she said, baffled by his anger, which seemed to be directed at himself. "You haven't offended me or anything. Quite the opposite."

That statement apparently did nothing to improve his mood. "It's not okay. I had no right."

As Anne watched him stride away up Greenwich to his car, she wondered why in addition to sounding so grim, Rick had sounded so damned resigned.

It was just a kiss. She touched her lips, exhaled slowly.

"Who in the hell am I kidding?" she muttered.

She felt just as she had after Gidayu Hamaguchi had made contact for the first time: a tad nervous, a little concerned and a whole lot curious.

CHAPTER FIVE

RICK didn't call Anne the following week, even though he contacted Gidayu almost immediately and arranged for the DNA tests that would determine if Chisato and Anne were related biologically.

Instead, when he heard back from Gidayu that Chisato was more than happy to provide a DNA sample, Rick sent Anne a letter via courier to relay the necessary information and the location of a reputable laboratory. The act was cowardly, but he wasn't sure what he would say to Anne once he had her on the telephone. And he sure as hell wasn't going to take any chances by delivering the news in person. Not with that kiss replaying in a taunting loop through his head.

The explosion of desire he'd experienced the moment their mouths had fused had not come as a surprise. Hardly. He'd wanted Anne for as long as he'd known her. Yet, he'd always managed to keep that fact to himself, hiding it behind a facade of indifference.

He snorted now as he paced the length of his office. So much for all of his manufactured aloofness. He'd blown everything to bits with one earthshaking kiss.

Now he had to build his meticulously constructed wall again from the rubble, and something told him that doing so would be even more difficult the second time around.

In truth, if Anne were anyone but his boss's baby sister, and if Rick's interest in her were purely physical, he would have made a move a long time ago. He'd hardly lived like a monk as an adult, even if he had purposely steered clear of any serious entanglements with members of the opposite sex.

He'd never spent an entire night with a woman, even though he sometimes thought it might be nice to have someone snuggled up beside him during those long hours before dawn broke and the sun helped to chase away his loneliness. But too much could be read into waking up in the same bed, and he didn't want to give any woman the impression he had more to offer than a few hours of mutual enjoyment. He had enough respect for the women he'd dated over the years to be clear about his intentions before things progressed much beyond their front doorsteps.

He would never marry and, most importantly, he would never have children. It was bad enough that Lester Danton's blood flowed through Rick's veins. No way was he going to pass on such dubious DNA to another generation and create the potential for a repeat of the hell he'd lived through as a child.

There were such things as monsters. Rick knew this firsthand. They didn't have frothing fangs or hide in closets and under beds. No. They sold insurance and looked deceptively normal as they sat at the head of the dinner table in the evening. They smiled as they asked about your day at school and then they stood to blacken your mother's eye because the mashed potatoes were too lumpy. When you begged them to stop, they warned you to mind your own business or your turn would come next. And it would, too, even without provocation. So you huddled in your closet or in the space under the basement steps and prayed you wouldn't be found. But you always were, and so instead you prayed that one day you would be big enough, strong enough, to fight back, to win.

A wave of nausea washed over Rick right along with the churned up memories. He passed a clammy hand over his face and swallowed the bile that rose in his throat.

Yes, he knew all about monsters. What sickened him the most was the knowledge that, ultimately, his father hadn't been the only monster in the Danton household.

He paced the length of his office again. Control. That was the key. Control and isolation would keep such monsters locked up. Control and isolation would ensure that the sins of the father were never visited upon another son.

Rick considered it his own brand of natural selection. And, in truth, it had been relatively easy to stay the course during the decade after college. Despite feeling lonely at times, he'd never been tempted to settle down. He'd never been interested in starting a family.

Until six years ago when he met Anne.

With her, basic sexual desire had quickly morphed into something a lot trickier. Even setting aside her kinship to J.T., Rick doubted that a brief, mutually sat-

isfying affair and an amicable parting of the ways
would be in the cards if he were to take Anne to bed.
No, he would want much, much more than that. He
would want exactly what he could not have. He would
want exactly what someone like him had no right to
expect let alone enjoy. That made his boss's baby sister
Rick's worst nightmare, even if she was also his
sweetest dream.

His telephone rang, interrupting his thoughts, and Rick
stalked to his desk to answer it. He'd been in a foul mood
for more than a week. It didn't improve when his executive assistant told him: "Miss Lundy is here to see you."

He raked a hand through his hair and sighed. Of
course she was. Her timing, as always, was lousy.

Even so, Rick's voice was as steady and confident
as ever when he told his assistant, "I'll see her, Mrs.
LeMott, but give me a minute before you send her in."

He combed his hair, shrugged into his suit coat and
straightened his tie. Anne walked through the door just
as he was pouring himself a cup of coffee from the in-
sulated carafe his assistant had brought in for a meeting
that was scheduled in fifteen minutes.

"Hi, Rick."

"Hello." He left off her name. Thanks to that kiss,
they were beyond the point—and the safety—of
courtesy titles, as Anne had insisted so vocally that afternoon on her porch. "Would you like some coffee?"

"Depends. Is it the real deal or is it decaf?"

"The real deal," he confirmed.

The smile that bloomed on her face nearly had him
dropping the carafe and forgetting his resolve.

"Sure. I'll take some then. I need a boost."

"You don't have enough energy?" he asked dryly as he selected a cup from the tray and filled it.

He'd never met anyone who was more animated or outgoing. He'd lay odds that Anne would burn more calories lazing on a beach than some people would pumping away furiously for an hour on a health club's StairMaster. The mental image of Anne reclining on the golden sand wearing a stingy scrap of a bikini popped front and center in his imagination and Rick felt perspiration dot his forehead.

After handing her the coffee, he surreptitiously wiped his brow with the back of his hand and took his seat.

Anne bypassed the chairs and settled one slender hip on the edge of his desk. Lucky mahogany, he found himself thinking, and yet he was nonetheless grateful for the width of polished wood that separated them.

"I didn't realize you were coming by today," he said politely as he leaned back in his chair. Distance. Control. "Did we have an appointment?"

Anne frowned. "No. No appointment. I was at Tracker to drop off some artwork that J.T. commissioned as a surprise for Marnie, and I figured while I was here I might as well stop in and follow up on our last conversation. Am I catching you at a bad time?"

He fiddled with his personal digital assistant, even though he had his schedule for the week committed to memory. "I have a meeting, but I guess I have a few minutes to spare for you before then."

"Gee, how flattering."

"Did you get the paperwork? I sent it by courier last week."

"I got it." She frowned again. "You know, you could have saved both time and money and just called me with the information." Her voice lowered and held just a hint of accusation. "You said that you would."

"I've been busy with work. Taking off time to spend that afternoon with you put me behind on some important Tracker business."

It was a lie, and not of the little white variety, either, but a complete fabrication. Oh, at first he had been a little behind schedule as a result of postponing his meeting. Since then, however, Rick had worked like a demon—not just for Tracker's benefit, but for his own. Falling in to bed dog tired each night was the most effective means he knew to keep his mind off things it had no business lingering over.

"You're not going to mention it, are you?"

"Mention what?"

"That...*interlude* on my porch." She sipped her coffee, holding his gaze over the rim of the cup. Something shimmered in her eyes. It appeared to be amusement along with, God help him, a dose of interest.

"It was just a kiss."

"Just a kiss?" She made a dismissive sound in the back of her throat. "I don't think it can be called that. What I gave you just before you left the first time was just a kiss. What you rushed back up the steps to give me was—"

"A mistake. I admitted as much at the time."

"I was going to say incredible," she contradicted with an easy smile.

"It's already forgotten," he lied in an effort to downplay what she was classifying as an interlude.

"Forgotten?" Her brows tugged together and her lips puckered in a way that had him compressing his tightly. "If that's the case, then I think I'm insulted."

"Sorry. Men and women approach these things differently, I guess."

"What things?"

"Hormones, chemistry." He shrugged.

"Are you talking about sex?"

His tie seemed to cut off his oxygen supply. Rick used his index finger to discreetly lever his collar away from his windpipe. The very last thing he wanted to talk about with Anne Lundy was sex.

"I'm just saying that it was an emotional day for you. I responded in kind, although I'll admit I crossed the line. But let's not confuse a…a mere gesture of comfort with sex," he said, pleased with his hasty explanation.

"I didn't confuse that kiss with the act of sex, any more than I would classify it as a 'mere gesture of comfort.'"

"Well, you're entitled to your opinion." He drummed his fingers on the desktop, hoping that was the end of it. Of course it wasn't.

"You're the one who likened it to sex," she added.

"What are you talking about?" His head began to thrum in rhythm with his fingers.

"That's what you just said. You said that men and women approach these things differently and when I asked what things, you said sex."

"No. I said hormones."

"And chemistry, I believe." She smiled. "And we both know what those can be euphemisms for."

"Why is it that every time we talk I wind up with a headache?" he asked. Of course, that wasn't the only part of his body throbbing just now.

Anne jiggled one foot and said nothing. He knew her too well to believe the silence would last. Sure enough, a moment later she was setting aside her coffee cup and asking bluntly, "So, that toe-curling kiss we shared was just to make me feel better about the situation with my birth mother?"

She sounded skeptical rather than hurt. That couldn't be a good sign. Rick didn't want her to be either, but if he had to pick one, then hurt would have at least bought him some distance. He decided to redirect the conversation along the tangent she provided.

"Well, did it take your mind off things?"

"It depends on what *things* you're talking about."

She raised her eyebrows meaningfully as she spoke and Rick felt the remnants of control further fray. Summoning up a look of indifference, he replied, "Not to be rude, but is there a point to this visit? Remember, I'm on your brother's dime right now."

"Actually, yes, there is a point. The lab called first thing this morning." She took a deep breath and the bravado she'd displayed a moment earlier evaporated. Her voice was a little reedy when she told him, "The results of the DNA test are back already."

"I see. That was fast." Of course, Rick had pressed the people at the lab to expedite things. He leaned forward in his seat. "And?"

"And I don't know. I'm on my way there now. They said they could give them to me over the phone or drop them in the mail even, but I didn't want to wait and I didn't want to hear whatever news is coming from some impersonal, disembodied voice." She cleared her throat and when her gaze connected with his again Rick saw vulnerability in her dark eyes. "In my head, I know what they're going to reveal, but…"

"You don't want to be alone when you hear it."

"No."

Her family was still in the dark. That left Rick as her sole emotional support.

Before he could answer her, though, his assistant knocked and then opened the door. "Mr. Danton, Craig Wyman and Josie Lowe from accounting are here for your meeting," she said.

He glanced at Anne, who scooted off his desktop and tugged at the hems of her layered tank tops.

"It's okay. You're busy. I…I can go by myself. Like I said, it's not as if anything they tell me will come as a huge surprise. I'll call you later. Let you know what I hear."

"Anne!"

Rick rushed around the desk and clasped her upper arm before she managed to clear his office door.

"If you can wait half an hour, I'll be happy to accompany you." As he spoke he slid his hand down until their palms pressed together and their fingers linked. So much for distance, he thought, before saying, "I want to be there for you."

"Thanks, Rick." She squeezed his hand and her eyes

grew bright as she confessed, "It's funny, given that you and I rarely see eye to eye on much of anything—hell, we couldn't even agree on the nature of that kiss—but I always know I can count on you. You're a good man."

He didn't say anything, although he was deeply touched. He simply didn't trust himself to speak.

"You're awfully quiet," Rick noted as they drove back to Tracker from the lab.

"I know. A lot on my mind."

"Are you okay?"

"Oh, I'm fine. I'm…just dandy." Anne waved the envelope clutched in her hand and beads tinkled in mocking merriment.

At the lab a kindly staff member had sat down with them to explain how the various markers unique to every person's DNA helped determine with a 99.9 percent probability that Anne and Chisato were close blood relatives. Anne had figured as much and so she'd thought she was prepared to hear her hunch confirmed. It turned out that one was never prepared to receive such news.

Her birth mother was alive. But while Chisato's long search had ended finally, Anne's quest for answers had just begun.

Surprisingly, she hadn't anticipated that.

Oh, there had been a time during her teen years when Anne had felt confused about who she was and how she had come to be with the Lundys. Most adoptees experienced those types of feelings at one time or another, or so she'd been told. That was often true in cross-cultural adoptions, where blending in to one's new family was not so easily achieved.

Anne had come to the Lundys when she was two years old and, to their credit, they had gone to great lengths to educate her about her birth mother's culture, even taking a month-long vacation to Japan the summer Anne turned fifteen. J.T., whiz that her brother was with languages, had been practically fluent in Japanese by then, but Anne had not been interested in learning more than a few cursory phrases. Perhaps it was foolish, but as a kid she had felt foreign enough already. She'd just wanted to be plain old American, not part of any hyphenated subset. She'd just wanted to fit in.

Now, some of the old questions returned, as well as some new ones. It troubled Anne greatly that something as random as chance had played such a large role in her life. But it was impossible to ignore the fact that if Roger Hastings had not snatched Anne from Chisato and brought her to the United States, Anne's entire life would have played out differently. She would be Ayano Hastings, the daughter of divorced parents and a citizen of Japan.

But *because* Hastings had taken Anne to the United States and then died so tragically, and *because* her paternal grandparents had made the coldhearted decision to pull strings and place Anne for adoption rather than return her to Chisato, and *because* Ike and Jeanne had decided they wanted another child and turned to adoption, she was Anne Lundy.

Different scenarios swirled in her head. What if Chisato had learned the truth sooner and found her daughter before the adoption could occur? Or, what if

Chisato had found Anne a couple of decades ago when Anne was still a minor?

Anne tortured herself now by wondering which mother would have stepped back, which one might have given up. And, if neither, what then? Would there have been a lengthy trans-Pacific custody battle that would have wrought bitterness and heartache before the final legal appeal was decided? And what might the final decision have been? Who would she be today: Anne Lundy or Ayano Hastings?

She massaged her temples as the beginnings of a headache throbbed. No matter how she approached it, one thing remained clear: Any disruption in the early chronology of her life would have changed its entire course dramatically. That thought made her feel as if she had no control, as if she had no say, not only in the child she had been but in the woman she had become.

She didn't like that. Not one bit.

"When we were kids, J.T. and I were horsing around in the living room one Saturday afternoon and we broke a vase that belonged to our mom," she mused quietly, tracing a fingertip over the letters of her last name, which was typed on the outside of the envelope. "That vase was Mom's favorite and we knew we'd catch hell if she found out, so instead of just coming clean, we glued the pieces back together as best we could."

"And?"

"Mom knew, of course. Forget the fact that it couldn't hold water, that vase didn't look the same. That's what this situation reminds me of, Rick. I have the feeling that nothing in my life will ever be the same again."

"That's because it won't be."

It wasn't necessarily what she wanted to hear, but Anne appreciated the fact that he didn't try to placate her or make false promises. No, he spelled it all out starkly with his next words. "The truth is some events cleave our lives into 'before' and 'after.' There's no way around that, even if we wish like hell that there was."

His tone seemed angry even as it also held a surprising amount of acceptance.

"You sound as if you're speaking from experience," Anne commented and turned to study his profile.

A muscle twitched briefly in his jaw, but he said nothing. He stared straight ahead and drove. It was a moment before he spoke again and when he did his tone was so matter-of-fact Anne thought she must have imagined its earlier edge.

"Not everything is outside your control, even if it seems that way right now. Ultimately you decide your future, Anne. What happens next isn't up to Gidayu or Chisato or even your parents. It's up to you."

She sighed, rubbed her eyes. "God, I wish I felt as empowered as you make me sound."

"You are."

"Okay, assuming it is up to me, why is it that I don't have a clue what I'm supposed to do next?"

"Well, it's not like this kind of thing comes with a manual," he said. "Give it time. You don't have to make any decisions right this minute."

"You're probably right, Rick."

"Now there's something I never thought I'd hear." He chuckled dryly.

"What?"

"You admitting that I'm right."

"Actually there's no cause to get smug. I said you were *probably* right," Anne clarified. Grinning, she added, "Everyone gets lucky from time to time."

She was happy to fall back into the bickering banter that long had characterized their relationship. After all, so much of her life was in upheaval. She wasn't quite ready to explore the whys and hows of her evolving feelings for Rick, even if she could acknowledge that things had definitely changed.

They drove in silence for a couple of minutes, then she said, "I guess I need to talk to Gidayu."

"I'll make copies of the lab report and fax it to him this afternoon."

"I'm sure it won't come as a surprise to him, either, but I think I should deliver the news in person."

"I'll see that he's informed. I can swing by his hotel on my way home from the office this evening."

Anne held firm. "No. I want to do it. I have questions about Chisato and, well, he did come all this way on her behalf. I want to meet him."

"Then I'll go with you."

"That's not necessary. His English seems fine from what I recall of our telephone conversations," she said. "I'll call his hotel and see if he is available for dinner."

"This evening?"

"No time like the present." She frowned then. "I believe it's important to have all of my facts straight before I drop a bombshell like this on my mom, dad and J.T. And I don't want to keep this from them any longer.

They're already phoning regularly and stopping in at my apartment to see if I'm okay."

"That's probably the smart thing to do." He nodded. "Make reservations for the three of us for seven o'clock." This time the steel in his tone matched her own.

"You're not still worried this could be a scam?" Anne asked, frowning.

"Not really. No," he admitted slowly. "My gut tells me Chisato and Gidayu are after nothing more than what they say they are—finding you and then perhaps establishing a relationship. But I can't completely discount that they might be after something more now that they know who you are. A positive DNA match to Chisato notwithstanding, you, Anne, remain the sister of one very wealthy and successful businessman."

"Better safe than sorry?"

"Exactly."

They pulled into Tracker's parking lot and Rick maneuvered his car to where Anne had parked her Miata.

"Thanks again, Rick," she told him, opening her door and getting out before he had a chance to unbuckle and perform his gentleman's routine for her. Leaning down, she added, "See you tonight."

He frowned across the empty seat at her. "I'll pick you up at six-thirty."

"That's okay. I can meet you at the restaurant. I'll call you with the name and location after I contact Gidayu."

"No, I'll call you. Six-thirty, Anne. Be ready."

CHAPTER SIX

AS PROMISED, Rick picked her up at six-thirty, arriving promptly and looking undeniably handsome in his usual neat charcoal gabardine, crisp white shirt and perfectly knotted necktie. Such conservative attire had never appealed to Anne in the past, but her taste seemed to be changing.

A *lot* of things were changing, she amended, when her heart temporarily knocked out an extra beat at his sardonic half smile.

"How do I look?"

Her dress was a simple, sleeveless cocoa-colored number whose pencil skirt ended at the knee. The neckline, while hardly plunging, hinted at the handiwork of the cleverly constructed under-wire she wore beneath it. She'd worn the dress a couple of times in the past and knew it was as comfortable as it was flattering. At the moment, however, she felt oddly self-conscious.

And that was before Rick's gaze dipped all the way to the three-inch heels strapped onto her feet and skimmed up slowly.

"Well?"

He glanced away and she swore it sounded as if he issued an oath.

"Rick?"

"The dress is a little…a little…" He frowned.

"Go on." Anne gestured for him to continue even though his dubious tone had her ego sinking. "It's a little what?"

"Just *little*." He ran a hand over the back of his neck. "Got anything that hits you at midcalf or so? Maybe something with a, um, turtleneck?"

Anne rested her hands on her hips and temper helped her bruised ego to rally. "What's wrong with this dress?"

"Nothing."

"Damned right there's nothing wrong with it. Marnie bought it for me for my last birthday, and I don't think you can fault her taste."

This was just one of the many offerings for petites in her sister-in-law's mail-order catalog business.

"I'm not faulting Marnie's taste," Rick said carefully.

"Are you saying I don't look good in this dress?"

"Anne—"

But she was too riled up to let him finish.

"I think I look good. *Damned good!* Do you have any idea how much chocolate I've had to avoid so this and all of the other outfits in my closet continue to fit me the way they're supposed to?"

It sounded as if he muttered, "Oh, it fits you all right."

That salved her pride some. Just to be sure, though, she asked, "Can you repeat that?"

"I said you look all right."

Anne gritted her teeth. "Gosh, Rick, you really shouldn't gush like that. You'll give me a big head."

He captured her chin between his thumb and index finger. "You're lovely, Anne."

Three words and they stole her breath. She felt herself flush, ridiculously flattered. It was a moment before she was able to murmur, "Thank you."

But, of course, Rick then ruined everything by qualifying the compliment. "I just think you should wear something a little more casual this evening."

The warm, fuzzy feeling she'd been experiencing chilled and turned prickly. "You're wearing a suit and tie," she pointed out. It dawned on her then that she'd never seen him in anything but corporate attire. Not that he didn't wear it well, but did the man own clothes that weren't tailored and didn't require dry cleaning?

"Okay, then, a little less…festive."

"You call brown cotton jersey festive?" God, the man acted as if she were wearing some saucy red sequined number that ended at midthigh.

"Demure then," he bit out. His gaze detoured again to the gentle swell of flesh that Anne proudly thought of as cleavage.

"Demure, hmm?" She crossed her arms under her chest in a move that further boosted her meager assets and gave her the satisfaction of watching Rick's Adam's apple bob just above his tidy Windsor knot. "I'm an artist. I don't do demure. Besides, I'm going to a restaurant to meet someone who was sent here by my biological mother. I'm not some debutante heading off to a cotillion. This dress is neither too flashy nor inappropriate for dinner at Claudio's on the Bay."

"For all practical purposes, this is a business meeting."

"It's not about business, Rick. It's about family."

"You know what I mean, Anne. You've never even met Gidayu Hamaguchi."

"Are you worried about first impressions?" She frowned then. "Do you think he'll have a problem with the way I'm dressed?"

"Maybe." He gestured vaguely and glanced away. "It's a, um, cultural thing."

She almost wavered then. The sad truth was that Rick knew far more about Japanese culture and customs than Anne did. But something about the muscle that twitched in his jaw, belying his bland expression, raised her suspicions. Was he…jealous? And, what did it say about her, she wondered, that she really liked that possibility?

"How old is Gidayu?" she asked. "You never did say."

Rick had met the man. What's more, Anne had little doubt he'd conducted a thorough background check on him as well.

"I don't know. Besides, what does it matter how old he is?" He was scowling.

Anne shrugged. "Just ballpark it for me."

"He's…fiftyish. Or so."

"Really? He sounded younger on the telephone."

Rick tapped a finger to the face of his watch mean-ingfully. "Anne, we really don't have time for a conver-sation here."

"So, you think I should change?"

She swore he sighed. "Yes."

"Well, that's just too bad." She patted his cheek before turning to collect a crocheted shawl and her handbag from the small table near the door.

She expected Rick to argue. Instead he shrugged as if conceding defeat. He took the wrap from her hands and laid it gently around her shoulders, ever the gentle-man.

"Thanks."

But he wasn't done. After tugging the fringed ends together he tied them tightly in a knot across her chest. Glancing up, he met her eye and coughed. "It's a little chilly out. Ready?"

Anne untied the shawl and weaved her arm through his. "Ready? No. But let's go anyway."

When they reached the restaurant, two things struck Anne immediately. First, Gidayu Hamaguchi was much younger than the "fiftyish" Rick had claimed him to be. And, secondly, he was quite good-looking.

He wasn't as tall as Rick or as broad through the chest, but he definitely did justice to the tailored camel sports coat he'd paired with trim black trousers. His tie, she noted, had one of her favorite cartoon characters dancing down the center of it. Along with the creases fanning out from his eyes, it hinted at a good sense of humor. For that reason alone, she liked him on sight.

"It is an honor to finally make your acquaintance, Miss Lundy," he said after bowing.

"It's nice to meet you, too." Then she couldn't resist adding, "You're a lot younger than I was expecting."

She glanced at Rick. He was not smiling. In fact, his expression bordered on dour.

"And you are more beautiful," Gidayu said.

"Call me Anne, please."

"Anne." He smiled warmly. "And you can call me Gid. It is…a nickname from college."

"Would that be Harvard or law school at Waseda?" Rick asked casually.

Gid's grin widened. "You are very thorough, Mr. Danton. Of course, I assumed you would investigate not only my client, but me as well."

"I hope you're not insulted," Anne inserted hastily.

The two men exchanged assessing looks, but Gid's expression held no bitterness when he glanced back at Anne. In fact, he seemed slightly amused. "I am not insulted. Were I in Mr. Danton's place, I would have done the same thing."

"You can call him Rick."

Gid's gaze slid to Rick, whose silence bordered on rudeness. Anne was considering how best to give him a discreet poke with her elbow when the maître d' arrived to show them to their table.

They were seated at the rear of the restaurant, near a window that boasted a lovely view of the bay. Rick pulled out Anne's chair and even though she had removed her wrap, the moment she was seated he returned it to her shoulders. Once again he pulled the crocheted fabric together below her chin, although this time instead of tying it he tossed an end over one of her shoulders.

"Air-conditioning is a little high in here," he commented. "I wouldn't want you to catch a chill."

"I'm fine."

Anne shrugged off the wrap and immediately felt cool air blast against her bare shoulders. Glancing up she saw a vent in the ceiling just behind her. Rick, who had taken his seat, smiled knowingly.

"You do these things on purpose, don't you?" she murmured.

"What things?" he asked innocently. But the crooking of his eyebrow told her he'd known perfectly well that the chair he'd selected for her was below that vent.

Anne decided to ignore the breeze. Surely the air would switch off soon. Besides, what were a few goose bumps when compared to her pride?

Their server came by a moment later and took their beverage order. When the young man withdrew, Rick turned to Gid, and Anne's hope that his previous line of questioning had been dropped was quashed quickly.

"My investigation turned up nothing disturbing on either you or Mrs. Nakanishi, and of course blood tests have since confirmed her claim to be Anne's biological mother. But I'm sure you can understand that I won't take any chances where Anne is concerned." Rick cleared his throat then and his gaze glittered hard. "Or her brother. Perhaps you've heard of him?"

"You refer to Jonathan Thomas Lundy, CEO and

founder of Tracker Operating Systems." The corners of
Gid's mouth tightened as he added, "Worth billions in
American dollars, I believe."

"Yes."

"And so you are wondering if Chisato Nakanishi is
after more than a reunion with the daughter who was
stolen from her. You are wondering if she is after money."

"Oh, please," Anne muttered on a sigh. Surely Rick
could employ some tact and diplomacy. He was going
for the jugular here. What was his problem? "I'm sorry,
Gid. Rick, can I speak to you for a moment in private?"

Rick didn't answer her, but Gid did. "No need to be
embarrassed."

"Well, just for the record," Anne said, "I don't
believe Chisato is after money."

"Your mother is, how you would say, financially
comfortable. She has worked hard throughout her life
and made prudent choices."

"How well do you know your client?" Rick asked.

"Very well."

"Oh?"

"She is the friend of my mother. I have known her
all of my life. Chisato is an honorable woman," he told
Anne. "She has no wish for money. She has no wish to
upset the Lundy family. She holds no anger or—how
would you say?—*ill will* toward the Lundys in this
matter. She is…" His lips again pursed thoughtfully
before he finished with, "Grateful."

"Grateful?" Rick asked.

"Yes, she is grateful that people as kind and respected
as the Lundys adopted Ayano and gave her a good home."

"Speaking of my parents," Anne said. "I haven't yet told them about Chisato. I wanted to know for certain if she was my birth mother before going to them."

"Your desire to protect them is most admirable."

"I need to know what Chisato wants exactly. I assume she wants to meet me," Anne said, and though she hadn't reached for Rick's hand, she felt it curl around hers on the tabletop.

Gid glanced at their linked fingers and back at Rick before his gaze returned to Anne. "Chisato is eager to see you again."

It didn't escape Anne's notice that while she spoke of meetings, Gid spoke of reunions—for Chisato had memories of the baby Anne had been whereas Anne had none of the mother who had brought her into the world and cared for her for nearly two years.

"Wh-when? And where?"

"She has asked me to tell you that the time and place are to be of your choosing. And, although she of course hopes differently, she will understand if you decide not to see her at all."

"I want to see her." Anne replied quickly. "I mean, she deserves that much after everything she's been through."

She would do this for Chisato's benefit, not her own. For some reason, that distinction seemed an important one. After all, if Anne's reasons were personal, wouldn't that make her disloyal somehow to Jeanne Lundy?

Gid smiled and nodded. "Chisato will be most pleased."

Their drinks arrived then and the waiter took their order. When he was gone, Anne asked quietly, "Has she been...happy?"

"She found happiness, yes."

"You mentioned that she's doing okay financially and I know she went to college. What does she do for a living?" Another thought came to her then. "Did she ever marry again?"

Rick and Gid exchanged a glance.

"Chisato remarried a few years after the divorce and everything else that transpired," Rick said. "Unfortunately her husband is no longer living. He died a few years ago."

"You knew this and didn't tell me?" Anne accused.

"We didn't know for certain until today that she was your birth mother. I figured you had enough on your plate without pondering the possibility of an extended family."

The truth hit her then. "My God! She has other children!"

"She has another child. A daughter," Rick said quietly.

"I have a half sister." Anne's heart did a somersault in her chest.

Rick's voice was pitched low and for her ears only. "I'm not going to have to shove your head between your knees again, am I? It's not a particularly flattering position, especially when you're wearing a dress."

Leave it to Danton to say something provoking. She tugged her hand from his. "I can't believe you knew all this and didn't tell me." Turning to Gid, she peppered him with questions. "What is she like? What's her name? How old is she?"

"Her name is Izumi. She turned twenty-five last spring."

"I assume someone told her about me," she said, shooting Rick another nasty look.

"Yes and Izumi is eager to meet you." He tipped his head to one side. "Of course, that meeting will be your decision as well."

Over the course of their meal, Gid politely answered all of Anne's many questions, as well as regaling her with stories of her relatives in Japan. Rick was silent and watchful.

Just before leaving the restaurant, Gid said, "I will be most happy to meet with you again if you think of other things you want to know."

He handed her his card, on the back of which was written the name and number of his hotel.

"I don't think Anne will need to meet you again," Rick said.

"What Mr. Danton means is that I will call you if I have any questions," Anne replied evenly.

"I believe I know exactly what Mr. Danton means," Gid replied and his grin held a challenge when he glanced at Rick. Turning back to her, he asked, "Can you speak Japanese, Anne?"

"No. I...I never learned more than a few cursory phrases." For the first time in her life, she truly regretted that. "My brother is fluent, though, and so is Rick."

"Yes. He speaks it very well," Gid agreed. "In Japan, we have a saying that sums up what Mr. Danton means."

In a low voice he rattled off something in his native tongue that had Rick lurching forward in his seat and issuing what sounded like a terse rebuttal. Anne couldn't understand the text of his reply, but based on his tone alone, she could tell he was angry. Gid said something else. Only the word Ayano was familiar. Rick was scowling. This time, his reply was less heated, but, whatever it was he'd said, he'd sounded no less resolute.

Anne rapped her knuckles on the linen-covered tabletop to gain their attention.

"Um, guys, mind speaking English here? I'm feeling a little left out."

"So sorry to be rude." Gid bowed.

"Yes, well, what was the saying that you mentioned?"

"It doesn't translate into English," Rick said crisply, his gaze locked onto Gid's. "At least not in a way that would make it…understandable."

A long pause ensued before Gid inclined his head once again. "My apologies, Anne. Mr. Danton is correct."

Anne waited until they were in Rick's car and driving home before she said: "What in the hell was that all about?"

"Nothing."

"Nothing? Please."

"Drop it, Anne."

She exhaled loudly. "You're just lucky I have other things to worry about right now than your amazingly rude behavior." She exhaled again. "I want to go to Japan to meet Chisato."

"You want to go there?" He seemed surprised.

"Yes." America was the domain of Jeanne Lundy. As irrational as it might be, Anne decided that if she could keep her two mothers in separate countries and divided by an ocean, then perhaps the situation would be easier for everyone to accept.

"I've been to Japan before," she murmured after a moment. "A long time ago now."

The Lundys had spent three weeks on the main island of Honshu, where they'd stayed in Tokyo, Yokohama and Osaka. They had not gone to Hokkaido, the northern-most island where Chisato now lived.

"A family vacation?" Rick asked.

"Yes. My mom and dad thought it was important for me to understand and appreciate the culture."

Her parents had not wanted her to lose touch with the roots Anne had always claimed to have no use for. They'd never hidden anything about her adoption from her, encouraging her to ask questions and seek answers. What had Anne done? For the past week she had skulked around, avoiding her mother's phone calls and swearing Rick to secrecy. She'd told herself she was doing it for her family's own good. She'd told herself there was no sense in upsetting them before she had all the facts.

Now, she could only hope they would see it that way.

"I've got to tell my parents." She blew out a gusty sigh and glanced at Rick. "I don't know what I'm going to say to them."

"The facts will do," he said simply, but she swore he sounded almost wistful when he added, "They love you, Anne, and they'll continue to love you no matter what. This won't change how they feel."

As before, Rick insisted on walking her to the door of her apartment. She felt anticipation building with each stair she scaled to the Victorian's front porch. Would he kiss her again? Would it be as earthshaking as the last time? And, if so, would he have the nerve to once again try to pass it off as a mere gesture of comfort?

He held out his hand and she gave him the key.

"You know, after having met Gid, I think I could have gone alone. He's a nice man. And he looks incredibly youthful…for his age."

Rick coughed and then grumbled, "I've never been good at guessing people's ages."

"You don't like him."

"I respect him," Rick said slowly.

"Well, I believe him."

"There's no reason not to," he conceded at last, holding open the door.

But Anne didn't step inside. "And yet you still got into it with him in Japanese."

"I thought we'd dropped that?" His tone suggested exasperation.

She shrugged. "Picking it back up again. Keep up, will you?"

"It was nothing."

"Oh, please. And don't give me that crap about how

whatever it was you two were talking about doesn't translate into English."

"It doesn't concern you."

"*Everything* about this situation concerns me, Rick. I *am* this situation. So don't you dare stand there and patronize me."

"Fine. We had a disagreement. Gidayu made an assumption about…me that I took issue with."

"An assumption about *you?*" Why did she get the feeling there was much more to it than that? "Well, even in another language, it came through loud and clear that you were upset. So, what was this assumption?"

Rick shook his head. "It doesn't—"

"Concern me?" she finished for him, arching her brows.

He said nothing.

"I heard my name, Rick. My Japanese name. You guys were talking about me. How can you say it doesn't concern me?"

"Leave it be, Anne," he said quietly.

"Just tell me what was it and I will."

"It's not something I'm comfortable repeating to you. He was off base and I told him so. Can we just leave it at that? Please."

Her curiosity was good and stoked now, but she backed down. What choice did she have when he sounded so…sad?

He was off base and I told him so.

What was Gid off base about?

"Be sure to lock your door when you get inside," Rick said, handing her back the key.

"I'll set the alarm, too," she said dryly. "I'm not a fool, Rick, nor am I a child."

He snorted. "I know that, Anne. Believe me, life would be a hell of a lot simpler for me if you were."

She angled her head to one side and let the shawl dip off her shoulders. "How so?"

He watched her for a long moment before pulling the shawl back up. "You can make kids listen."

Anne shrugged. "Well, even though I could have gone by myself tonight, thanks for coming with me."

"You're welcome."

He pushed the door open a little wider, almost as if he were eager for her to go inside, but Anne leaned against the jamb.

"You know, I seem to find myself thanking you a lot lately."

"That's because I'm such a nice guy," he said lightly.

"You camouflage it well enough, but yes," she conceded. "And so I am in your debt."

"That's not where I want you, Anne."

"Where do you want me?"

She wasn't sure what answer she had expected to such a loaded question. God, she couldn't believe she'd asked it. Rick said nothing, almost as if he was already regretting his comment. The moment stretched along with the silence. Then the young couple who rented the downstairs apartment turned up the walk, chattering noisily.

"Good night, Anne."

Before she could even tell him the same, Rick had disappeared into the foggy night.

Where do you want me?

Rick sat in his car and waited for his breathing to even out. He could think of about a dozen answers, all of them erotic, none of them remotely possible when it came to Anne and him.

You're no better than your father.

Those words rang in his head. It was what his mother had told him on that fateful night a couple dozen years earlier when his world had split into before and after. It was the last thing she'd said to him as police and emergency medical technicians arrived at their home, the lights on their vehicles flashing, their sirens blaring. The words had cut more deeply than the gash his father's fist had split open on Rick's hairline.

Rick had thought she would thank him for standing up to the old man and freeing her—freeing them both—from Lester Danton's brutality. But she'd stood there in her ripped and bloodied nightgown and shrieked at him.

You're no better than your father!

As mistreated as his mother had been, it turned out that the thing Miriam Danton feared most was not her abusive husband, it was being alone. They had barely spoken since that day.

Well, Rick wasn't afraid of being alone. In fact, he'd long ago determined that alone was the best place for someone like him to be. Yet as he watched the light switch on in what he knew to be Anne's bedroom, he found himself wishing he could be wrong.

CHAPTER SEVEN

ALL of the Lundys—including Marnie, J.T. and Noah, Marnie's young son from her first marriage—were seated around Ike and Jeanne's dinner table the following evening. Anne had asked for a family meeting and, last minute though her request was, they all had complied, curious if not anxious to finally hear the explanation behind Anne's recent uncharacteristic evasiveness.

The scene in the dining room was so Norman Rockwell-ish that Anne nearly sighed. Irish linen was spread over the table, which was heaped with enough food to feed twice their number and set with the china Jeanne and Ike had received as a wedding gift more than forty years earlier. Her mother always pulled it out for special occasions. These days, with J.T. remarried and Anne busy with her photography, getting the extended Lundy clan around the same table qualified as a special occasion, especially since Anne had been dodging her mother's phone calls.

"More polenta?" Jeanne asked, holding out a steaming serving dish.

"No thanks, Mom."

At one time Jeanne had had a cook—a bona fide, French-trained chef. J.T. had paid the man an obscene amount to hire him away from one of the swankiest restaurants in New York City. He hadn't wanted their mother to lift a finger during her retirement years. It had taken less than a month for Jeanne to give the guy the boot. Her son might be a billionaire, but she preferred to prepare meals herself, thank you very much. The kitchen was her domain. Trying new recipes and experimenting with herbs and spices provided a creative outlet, which she found to be cathartic.

Hence, tonight's meal, Anne thought, feeling another sharp twinge of guilt as her gaze took in the stuffed pork tenderloin, herbed polenta, roasted mixed vegetables and steamed asparagus. She spied Noah covertly stuffing half a dozen green spears beneath the rim of his plate and winked at him. Poor kid. Marnie had made it clear he needed to finish his vegetables or there would be no dessert.

Anne glanced at the half-dozen green spears that remained on her own plate and was thankful to be an adult, since Jeanne had made black forest cherry cake. It was Anne's favorite. She sighed. Sometimes, things as small and seemingly insignificant as dessert provided the glue that helped hold her together. This was *her* family. It would always be *her* family. Even if she also needed to journey to a distant land to meet other people who could claim her as kin.

She glanced over, intercepting her mother's worried frown, and her heart twisted. It was time to explain ev erything. Setting aside her fork and knife, she cleared her throat to gain their attention.

"I'm sure you're all wondering why I wanted to see you tonight," she began.

J.T. shrugged. "Not especially. Mom said she was making stuffed pork tenderloin. That was a good enough reason to get me here."

Anne didn't need to send him a black look. Her father did that at the same time Marnie gave him a sharp poke in the ribs with her elbow.

"Go on, dear," Jeanne coaxed.

"I know I've been a little evasive lately. I'm sorry about that." She smiled at her mom then. "*Really* sorry. It's just that I…I found out… Um, that is, I recently learned…"

Ike, being the practical sort, suggested: "Sometimes it's best just to spit it out all at once, Annie."

Her father was the only one who ever called her that. The nickname had tears threatening.

"Okay." Anne glanced around the table. Everyone, even young Noah, was watching her, waiting. Here goes nothing, she thought. "It turns out that my birth mother is alive and wants to meet me."

The truth detonated like a bomb, shattering the silence and setting off an explosion of questions that were hurled from all directions like jagged shrapnel. Anne had expected that, since she had plenty of questions herself.

"That's impossible!" Jeanne exclaimed. "You were an orphan when we got you."

"Are you positive this woman is really who she claims to be?" her father asked at the same time J.T. said, "It goes without saying that we'll have her investigated."

"I'm positive. DNA doesn't lie."

"DNA," Jeanne repeated slowly.

"I took a test. Rick Danton helped set it up. Chisato and I...well, we match up nearly perfectly."

"But where has she been all of these years?" Marnie asked.

"In Japan." Anne worried her lower lip and glanced at her parents. "She and my birth father were divorced. He was an American, just like you were told at the time of my adoption, but it seems that he took me to the United States without her permission or knowledge, and then he died unexpectedly."

"But why were you placed for adoption?" Marnie asked. "Why weren't you just returned to Japan?"

"I'm not sure," Anne admitted. "Although it seems that my birth father's parents weren't too pleased to have a granddaughter who is *haafu.*"

It was one of the few Japanese words Anne knew. It meant half Japanese and half Western, although it wasn't generally intended as a derogatory term.

Her father swore, right after which he turned beet-red and apologized. Wagging his index finger at Noah, he said sternly, "I'd better never catch you repeating what I just said, young man." Then he turned to Anne. "And you'd better not be letting someone else's small-mindedness weigh on you."

"Never, Dad," she said. "You and Mom raised me to know better than that."

He nodded briskly, but his eyes were moist. "They don't know what they've missed out on."

"But my birth mother does. She's…she's been looking for me ever since."

"Oh, that poor woman!" Jeanne's eyes filled with tears, which she wiped with her cloth napkin, unmindful of the smudges her mascara left on the linen. "I don't even want to imagine how devastated she's been, searching in vain."

"Until now," J.T. inserted.

"Yes, until now."

Her mother dabbed her eyes again. Marnie was sniffling as well, one hand resting protectively on her distended belly.

"It's so sad," her sister-in-law murmured. J.T. reached over to brush away his wife's tears.

"I don't think any of us can imagine what this woman went through. Nor can we imagine what you're feeling, Anne."

"Are you okay, Annie?" her dad asked.

Their obvious concern brought emotions bubbling back to the surface.

"I've never had much of a problem with being adopted. I've always known I was loved and wanted. But now that I know she's alive and that she didn't mean to give me up…I guess I feel confused…conflicted," she said at last, realizing the truth of those words as she glanced at her mother. "I didn't expect to feel this way."

Jeanne's smile was warm and reassuring. "How could you not be shaken up by this information, Anne? But for a quirk of fate you might not have been part of our family."

Silence followed that observation until Noah piped up.

"So, you could have been Japanese." The little boy

grinned, showing off a charming gap between his two front teeth. "That's so cool!"

He was not quite six years old, but he, too, already had learned some painful lessons about the seemingly random twists and turns life could take. His father had died in an accident when Noah was still in diapers and but for a quirk of fate his mother might never have met and married J.T.

"Actually, honey, she's always been part Japanese," Marnie corrected. Using her fork, she reached over to roll the asparagus spears from their hiding place beneath her son's plate. Noah groaned dramatically before slumping back in his chair.

"So, what now, Anne?" her brother asked. "You mentioned earlier that she wants to see you."

Anne glanced at her mother. "Yes. She's leaving the choice up to me. I get to decide when and where."

"I noticed you didn't say if. So, you're going to meet her?" J.T. asked.

"I…" Anne's gaze strayed to her mother again. Why did she suddenly feel so disloyal?

"Of course she's going to meet her," Jeanne said.

"Mom?"

"I want you to, Anne. You owe it to your birth mother after everything she's been through, but more importantly, you owe it to yourself." Jeanne stood then and glanced around at the table's silent occupants. "I made black forest cherry cake for dessert. I hope you all saved room."

When she was gone, Ike stood. "I think I'll just go help your mother."

Anne set aside her napkin and rose as well. "No, Dad. Let me."

Jeanne was at the granite-topped island, slicing up the cake, when Anne entered the kitchen. Her movements were sure and steady despite the arthritis that had disfigured her knuckles and required daily pain medication. She glanced up when Anne entered and smiled.

"I made this from scratch this afternoon even though the ones at that new bakery are nearly as good."

"Yours is my favorite," Anne said.

"I know," Jeanne replied on a wink.

"You've made it special for me for every big occasion in my life, not to mention each September 13th."

It was the day Anne had joined their family and the Lundys still celebrated it.

"That was one of the happiest days of my life." Jeanne laid down the knife then, covered her mouth and sobbed.

Anne was at her side in a moment, wrapping her arms around her mother in a fierce hug. "I won't meet Chisato. I won't."

Jeanne shook her head. "No, no. I want you to. Really. That's not why I'm crying."

"Then why?"

"I just feel so…guilty."

Her answer surprised Anne. "Guilty? What have you got to feel guilty about?"

"As much as I'm sorry for that poor woman and what she has gone through, I'm so glad you're part of our family. I'm so glad that even though she's been looking, she didn't find you while you were still a child.

How could I have given you up? Her greatest heartache became my greatest joy." She sobbed again. "What kind of a person does that make me?"

"Oh, Mom. You're the best. None of what happened is your fault."

"I know. It's not her fault, either." Jeanne took a moment to compose herself. Then she grasped Anne's elbows and held her daughter at arm's length. "Just wait until she meets you. She's going to be very proud when she sees what a fine, beautiful and talented young woman that baby she gave birth to has become."

"You did a good job, Mom."

"I had good material to work with." Jeanne patted Anne's cheeks, her thumbs wiping away the tears that dampened them. "She saw to that."

"I love you, Mom."

"I love you, too, sweetie." She stepped back then and straightened the blouse that was tucked into the waistband of her tailored slacks. "Goodness, we'd better get this dessert served. Noah is probably wondering what kind of grandma I am after serving steamed asparagus and then keeping him waiting for the best part of the meal."

Noah wasn't a Lundy by blood, either, but that didn't matter to Jeanne. She doted on the little boy and spoiled him as thoroughly as either of his other two grandmothers did. Her love knew no boundaries. It was not measured against any qualifications. She'd never asked for anything in return. And so as she helped transfer slices of cake onto small china plates Anne had to know.

"Are you sure it doesn't bother you that I'm going

to meet her?" she asked.

"Why should it bother me, Anne?"

"I don't know."

Jeanne set the knife in the sink, wiped her hands on the dish towel and laid it aside. "Do you think I should feel jealous? Or that maybe I should feel threatened?"

Anne scooped a little bit of frosting off the cake and licked it from her finger. Shrugging, she admitted, "I don't know."

"Oh, Anne." Jeanne smiled and reached for her daughter's hands. "Ayano," she crooned softly, three syllables that seemed as settling as a favorite lullaby coming from the woman who had raised her. "Someone else gave you life. That's a fact I can't change. She brought you into this world, but I brought you *up* in it. She and I played different roles. It's not a competition."

"But *you're* my mom," Anne stressed.

Jeanne smiled and pulled her in for a hug. "I'm your mom, Anne. Forever."

After dessert was eaten, the Lundys moved to the living room, where Anne told them everything she knew about Chisato Nakanishi. It still amazed Anne how easy it was to tell them about her other family. They seemed excited and curious, based on the many questions they asked and comments they made as she spoke.

"It turns out I also have a half sister. She's twenty-five," she told them.

She glanced at J.T., wondering what he thought of the matter. Her brother was grinning broadly, not thrown in the least by the news that he wasn't the only person who could now call Anne a sibling.

"You always wanted someone younger to push around. Looks like you got your wish."

For more than an hour, the conversation continued. It felt good, Anne realized, to have it all out in the open. She appreciated her family's advice. Even more, she appreciated the way they had all rallied around her with their support. She'd always known she could count on them, but they proved it again in spades.

"I'll go with you to Japan," J.T. said. "I've never been to Sapporo, but it's a large city. I'll book us some first-class accommodations. We'll take Tracker's jet. When were you thinking of leaving?"

Anne hadn't really considered a departure date, but the words "a week from Monday" had no trouble popping out of her mouth.

"I'll clear my schedule at work."

"No, J.T. I can't let you do that. I think you're needed here," she replied, nodding in the direction of her sister-in-law.

"The baby's not due for another two months, Anne. I can manage without my husband for a week or so. I'll be fine," Marnie assured her.

"No, I think Anne's right," Jeanne said. "You know, your father and I wouldn't mind seeing Japan again."

Anne wanted her parents there, but…she didn't. She couldn't quite explain it to herself. How was she going to articulate it to them without ruffling their feathers?

"That's sweet, Mom, really," she began slowly.

"You don't want us to go?"

"It's not that I don't want you to go. It's just that I…I…." Anne stammered miserably.

Ike saved her from continuing. "It's okay, Annie. I think I understand why you don't want us there for the initial meeting. But you shouldn't go alone."

"Yes, let J.T. accompany you," her mother said. "It would ease my mind knowing he was there, too, especially since he can speak the language."

"All right." She nodded. Glancing at Marnie, she added, "I won't be gone long. Probably a week."

"Or two," J.T. said with a smile.

Two? No. Well, maybe. "But you don't need to stay the entire time. Once I'm settled in and the introductions have been made, I'm sure I'll be fine."

She told them about Gidayu then and how well the man spoke English. And about all of the help Rick had been so far. J.T. seemed to watch her carefully as she spoke.

"Rick certainly can keep a secret," her bother mused. Something about his tone made her think he wasn't referring only to the matter with Chisato. But before she could wonder about it, Marnie was saying, "I'd love to come, too. Unfortunately my obstetrician has ruled out air travel at this stage in my pregnancy."

"I want to go to Japan." Noah pouted.

"Next time we'll all go," Jeanne promised the boy.

And it struck Anne then that there most likely would be a next time.

What was it Rick had said? Some events bisect one's

life into before and after. He'd spoken with such author-
ity that Anne couldn't help wondering now: What event
had changed things so cataclysmically for him?

CHAPTER EIGHT

ANNE had never been to Rick's house, but thanks to a discreet glance in her mother's address book she knew where he lived. Jeanne Lundy had a soft spot for the man, whom she always referred to as "a nice boy," even though he was in his late thirties. Anne's mother sent him a Christmas card every year.

Sure enough, Anne found his home address and telephone number listed in her address book, as well as his shirt size, hobbies and date of birth.

Hmm, a Taurus. The bull. Why wasn't *that* surprising?

Anne tried to call him from her cell phone after leaving her parents' house, but she got no answer. Disappointed, she nonetheless drove toward his neighborhood. She was too keyed up to go directly home. Maybe he would be in by the time she got there. It was after ten o'clock. Surely even a workaholic like Rick would kick back in an easy chair with the television remote at some point before midnight.

She drove slowly along Filbert Street, looking for the

house number that she'd scribbled on a piece of note-paper. It still surprised Anne that he lived here.

Oh, she knew her brother paid Rick well, so it was no shock he could afford a house in the pricey Telegraph Hill neighborhood. It was just that she found it odd that Rick Danton of all people would prefer a quaint, cottage-style home tucked amid eucalyptus trees and surrounded by lush gardens. Based on his long hours, she'd pegged him as a condo dweller. Or maybe even the inhabitant of an apartment in one of the city's modern high-rises. Neither of those choices required much upkeep or elbow grease.

Even in the dark, with just the lights sprinkled around the landscaped grounds, she could tell this place required tending. Of course, Rick could afford to hire out home repair and maintenance. Still, the man just kept surprising her.

After parking her car in the driveway, she grabbed the wrapped slice of her mother's cake from the passenger seat and walked to the front door. The lights were on inside, as was music. It was blasting away so loudly that even through the thick panel of oak she could make out clearly Bix Beiderbecke's cornet as it caressed each note. Anne smiled. It still amazed her that she and Rick had jazz in common.

She gave up after five minutes of pounding. Whatever the man was doing, he wasn't likely to hear her. She was pulling the keys back out of the front pocket of her black pants when she thought she heard the thudding of feet. Sure enough the volume on the music was lowered and then what sounded like a safety chain rattled. Rick wasn't the only one surprised when the door opened and they came face-to-face.

"Oh. You were working out," Anne said, amazed her tongue cooperated to form the words since it wanted to loll out of her mouth at the sight of him.

He made quite a picture in his damp tank-style T-shirt and gray cotton shorts. His face was flushed, beaded with perspiration from apparent exertion. His hair was messy and all the sexier for it.

"God, you're hot." She blinked, unable to believe she'd voiced that observation out loud. She just hoped he took it to mean his temperature. "Um, you know, sweaty from working out." Her gaze followed the line of perspiration that seemed to divide the front of his snug-fitting T-shirt in two. He had some impressive pectoral muscles filling out that soggy bit of cotton.

"Sweaty," she murmured a second time. "And…incredibly hot." Then she flushed again. Maybe she should just shut up.

One side of his mouth lifted. "Are you always this articulate?"

She focused on his face, determined not to humiliate herself again by letting her gaze detour to his nicely sculpted arms and shoulders. But then she was laughing.

"Give me a break. It's kind of hard to talk, not to mention stand, when you have both of your feet in your mouth."

He crossed his arms and studied the size five-and-half Jimmy Choos she was wearing. "Hmm. Must be hell on your throat. Those heels look downright lethal."

"And they cost a fortune, too." Anne shrugged. "I figured I'm worth it."

"Of course. So, what brings you to my door at this late hour?"

"I was just in the neighborhood."

"My neighborhood?" His eyebrows arched.

"I had dinner with my family tonight. That's sort of in this neighborhood."

In fact, it wasn't and they both knew it, but he didn't call her bluff. The truth was she didn't know what exactly had prompted her to come here. Yet, even as he stood there with that patronizing smile on his face, she was glad to see him.

"Ever hear of calling first?" he asked.

"This from the man who gave me five-minutes' notice before showing up at my door?" But then she waved her hand as if wiping the slate clean. "Actually I tried to call you. I didn't get an answer."

"And yet you decided to stop by anyway."

"What can I say? I'm a risk-taker by nature. Besides, I didn't feel like heading back to my apartment just yet. Too…restless. I figured I'd wear off some of this extra energy first."

He didn't say anything. But she wanted to believe that the muscle twitching in his jaw spoke volumes.

"I've been pounding on your door for five minutes, by the way," she told him.

"I guess my music was a little loud."

"What's the point of putting on Bix if you can't let his cornet make the windows rattle every now and again?"

"We're in perfect agreement."

"I'm sure it won't last."

"No." But he was smiling.

She glanced past him. "Are we going to carry on our entire conversation in your doorway or are you going to invite me in? It would be the polite thing to do, you know, since I come bearing both news and a gift."

She held out the foil-wrapped plate then, which he eyed speculatively.

"What exactly do you have under there?"

"My mom's black forest cherry cake. Made from scratch this very afternoon." She bobbed her eyebrows meaningfully. "It's almost as good as sex."

Rick seemed to hesitate.

"I won't bite," Anne promised.

After a long pause, he stepped back to allow her to enter. She was just brushing past him when he replied softly, "I might."

The teasing response had heat shimmying up her spine. Turning, she winked at him. "I guess I'll have to take my chances. Risk-taker, remember?"

He showed her into a living room that was surprisingly homey. Neither the walls nor the furniture's rich upholstery was relegated to the bachelor-pad beige she'd been expecting. They were done in surprisingly vibrant hues that seemed to confirm Anne's suspicion that a lot of passion was percolating beneath the man's generally reserved exterior. Her heart knocked unsteadily at the thought.

"Nice place."

"I like it."

"Decorate it yourself?"

He shrugged. "Sort of."

"Ah. That means you hired a professional," she said with a knowing smile.

"I still had to approve her selections," he pointed out. "I merely delegated the legwork."

"Well, I like her choices for over the mantel." Anne nodded toward the pair of framed nature prints that hung above the fireplace. "I'm a huge fan of Seth Ridley's. The guy is an enormous talent."

"I'm a huge fan as well," Rick said. "I picked those prints up at his first New York show. They've proven to be a good investment already. You can't touch anything of his now for what I paid for those."

"Well, you have good eyes."

The eyes in question regarded her solemnly. "I know what I like, Anne."

"And you go after it."

"Usually."

"Why not always, Rick?" Anne moistened her lips before continuing boldly, "I mean, if you *really* want something, why hold back?"

They were talking about more than art and they both knew it, yet he made no move to back up his previous words. She couldn't quite figure him out. She was sure he was attracted to her. That kiss on her porch had spelled it out plainly. But here they were, alone in his home with the double entendres flying, and…nothing.

"It's not as simple as that," he said at last.

"Why not?" It came out a whisper.

"It's…just not."

"Oh."

"Sorry."

The last thing Anne wanted at the moment was a damned apology. She swallowed hard and glanced around the room again. Forcing a smile to her lips she said, "God, Danton, you're disgustingly tidy."

"Some of us prefer order."

His tone brimmed with the same smug amusement that had always put her back up. She wondered if his use of it now was intentional. In any case, it certainly helped smooth away the awkwardness.

"Was that a polite way of saying I'm a slob?"

One side of his mouth lifted along with his broad shoulders. "If the red panties on the floor fit…"

"You know, I could be just as nosy as you were that day you stopped by my home unexpectedly. I bet if I poked my head into your room right now I'd find your bed unmade and personal things lying around on the floor.

"My room is as neat as the rest of my home."

"Care to make a wager on it?" She stuck out her hand.

She expected him to rise to the challenge, but he merely nodded.

"Point taken." Then he motioned toward the couch. "Why don't you make yourself comfortable while I grab a quick shower? I have Cole Porter coming on after Bix."

Anne waited until she heard the water running before she tiptoed down the hallway to his bedroom. She wasn't a snoop by nature, but she had to see proof of his disorderliness firsthand, even though his previous answer had seemed to confirm it.

Once inside, however, she frowned. The bed was made, and other than a shirt laid over the back of the chair under the window, the place was annoyingly neat. It surprised her that he hadn't marched her in here to show it off and prove her wrong. She turned, intending to leave quietly before he finished his shower in the adjoining bathroom, but the artwork over the bed's headboard caught her eye and shock rooted her in place.

She recognized the prints immediately, of course. They were hers. More precisely, they were the four prints from her lovers' series that had sold to an anonymous collector for a princely sum at her first gallery show.

Rick Danton was her anonymous collector? Why hadn't he just said so?

She heard the shower switch off then and hurried out of the room before she could be caught.

Rick stepped from the shower, shivering. The water hadn't been cold. It had been as close to freezing as he could stand. Even so, he still felt hot enough to combust. He couldn't believe Anne was in his house.

One minute he'd been working out, furiously lifting weights so that when he fell into bed later that evening he would be too exhausted to fantasize about her. The next minute, he'd opened the door to her smiling face and the elevated rate of his heart had had nothing to do with his previous physical exertion.

What had spurred the cold shower, though, wasn't her mere presence. No, it was her bold suggestion that if he really wanted something, he should go after it.

More than awareness, her dark eyes had held anticipation and, God help him, invitation. Rick had been so tempted to take her advice. To take *her* into his arms.

He toweled off vigorously now, cursing under his breath. If only it were that simple. Hell, if anything, his relationship with Anne just kept getting more complicated.

Being around the woman certainly had been much easier when she'd considered Rick heavy-handed and intrusive. She'd seen him more as an annoyance than as a man then, and even though that hadn't done much for his ego or his frustration level, at least it had provided a nice, safe buffer. Now, he got the feeling she even enjoyed their disagreements, perhaps because she also knew how much they actually had in common.

Rick pulled on a pair of jeans. For modesty's sake, he decided it was best to leave his shirt untucked. Inhaling deeply, he prepared to face her again.

"Would you care for a drink?" he asked when he returned to the living room. "I opened a nice red earlier this evening."

"Good God!"

"What? What is it?" he asked. The shocked look on her face as her gaze skimmed down his torso and then continued to his bare feet made Rick wonder if his arousal was still that damned obvious.

But then she smiled and her eyes crinkled with humor. "You own jeans, Danton. Actual denim."

"Everybody owns jeans," he grumbled. "So, do you want some wine or not?"

"Well, since you twisted my arm, sure." He was

halfway to the kitchen when she called, "And bring a fork for the cake. You've got to try it."

Better than sex, she'd said earlier. In the kitchen, he scrubbed a hand over his face and swallowed hard. As he filled two goblets with wine, he realized his hands were less than steady. He had to get her out of there. One glass of wine, a few bites of cake and then the door. That was the game plan.

Then he returned to the living room and he nearly forgot his own name. Did she have to look so lovely or smile so engagingly? She was seated on his couch, the cushion next to her looking more inviting than a prime seat at a football game. He handed her a glass of wine and went to sit in one of the chairs opposite her, grateful for the wooden coffee table that separated them.

Anne nudged the plate of cake in his direction.

"I see you brought chopsticks in addition to a fork." She made a face. "Show-off."

"Actually the chopsticks are for you." He leaned forward and handed them over.

"Me?"

"I have yet to meet a woman who doesn't nibble on a man's dessert even if she claims not to want any."

She frowned, looking slightly insulted, although she didn't argue his point. "Well, you could have at least brought me a fork. I'm not very good with those yet."

"I know. I figured you could use the practice and I could use the advantage."

He smiled and helped himself to a generous bite of cake. It was delicious, but what had him moaning was the fact that Anne had left the couch and was now settled on the edge of the sturdy wooden table. She was so close to him that their knees touched and when he inhaled, he could smell her. She always wore the same scent, and it never failed to tangle with his hormones.

"Sinful, isn't it?" she asked.

"Very."

"And irresistible," she added, trying to pick up a bite with the chopsticks. She gave up after a moment and commandeered his fork.

"Irresistible," he agreed as he watched her mouth close over the stainless steel. Afterward, she licked a stray bit of frosting from the side of the fork before handing it back to him.

"My mom always makes this special for me. For J.T., she whips up peach cobbler. For Dad it's pecan pie. But I'm black forest cherry cake."

The mention of her family helped Rick reel in his runaway libido. He cleared his throat.

"You said you were at your parents' for dinner. I assume you told them about Chisato."

"Yes. J.T., Marnie and Noah were there, too. I wanted to tell them all at once."

"How did it go?"

He knew the answer even before she responded. Something about Anne seemed more settled this evening. He imagined for someone as close as she was to her family, keeping secrets from them, even just for a couple of weeks, would have been difficult.

"Amazingly well, actually. They're very supportive of my decision to meet Chisato and my half sister."

"I knew they would be." Rick envied her that kind

of unconditional love. He'd never known it from his own parents. He picked up his wine and offered a toast. "To your families, Anne. Both the one here and the one you will soon meet in Japan. May they know how lucky they are to count you among their number."

She was smiling as she clanked her glass against his. "That's really sweet. To my families."

They drank their toast and then she asked, "What's your family like, Rick?"

It was a polite question, bordering on small talk, and yet it had his stomach knotting, his palms sweating. "Let's just say they're nothing like yours and leave it at that."

Anne eyed him curiously for a moment. "I'm sorry."

"Me, too."

She was waiting for him to expound. He couldn't, even though for the first time in years, he found himself actually wanting to. But, God, what would she think of him then?

He cleared his throat. "So, tell me about dinner."

"Well, J.T. has offered to come to Sapporo with me."

"I figured he would."

"And, of course, Gidayu Hamaguchi will be there."

That prospect had Rick grinding his back teeth, although he mustered up a thin smile. "I'm sure he'll be only too happy to offer his assistance should you need anything."

"Yes." She tilted her head to one side and studied him. "You know, I think Gid might have a crush on me."

He managed what he hoped was a look of bored indifference. "Oh? Why do you say that?"

She shrugged. "Just a feeling. You know how it is.

Sometimes you can just tell when someone is attracted to you, even if they try to hide it."

He cleared his throat and said nothing.

Anne had no problem filling the silence. "They give off these very definite signals."

"Do they?"

"Yes. *Very* definite signals." Her eyebrows rose slightly for emphasis. "As I said, sometimes those signals are camouflaged pretty well, but if you pay attention, you spot them eventually."

"And you picked up these signals from Gid during dinner the other night?"

"I definitely picked up *some* signals the other night." She used her index finger to scoop up some frosting, which she then licked off with her tongue and Rick's own mouth began to water. "But maybe I'm wrong. What do you think?"

She expected him to think right now?

He took a sip of wine, buying some time, and then he shrugged dismissively. "Well, I'm no expert."

Anne's laughter trilled. "That's never kept you from offering your opinion in the past, Rick."

He took another sip of wine and ignored the barb. "He's a man. Why wouldn't he be interested? You're a beautiful woman, Anne."

"Oh, so you think I'm beautiful?"

"I believe I've mentioned something to that effect before," he replied dryly.

"Yes." She grinned in full now. "You're a regular fountain of flattery. So, what did your investigators turn up on Gid?"

"Nothing damning. Yet."

"Still checking?"

His shrug was noncommittal, even though he most certainly was.

"Do you think Gid knows that I'm currently unattached?"

Rick didn't bother with a sip. He gulped his wine this time. "I have no idea."

Which was a lie. Indeed, he had more than an idea. At the restaurant the other night Gid had asked point-blank, although thankfully in Japanese, if Rick and Anne were a couple. He'd assumed as much, apparently picking up on the kind of signals to which Anne had just referred. When Rick had told the other man he was mistaken, Gid had asked if Anne knew Rick was in love with her. They had exchanged some heated words, Rick denying any interest and then Gid had asked if Anne were seeing anyone. Of course, Rick would roast in hell before telling her that.

"He seems very nice, don't you think? And, of course, he's good-looking."

"He's really not my type," Rick said dryly and willed his grip on the wineglass to loosen, lest he snap the stem in half.

"What is your type? I asked you once before but you never really told me. What kind of women do you date?"

"Blondes," he lied. "Tall ones, with a little extra meat on their bones."

"Ah. That's interesting."

He knew he would regret asking, but he did so anyway, "Why do you say that?"

"I don't know. It's just that that would be the polar opposite of me." She smiled as she said it, and her gaze held both amusement and challenge.

Rick finished off the last of his wine and remained silent.

"Well, it's not like you can help who you're attracted to," Anne added with a negligent lift of her shoulders. "You know what I mean?"

He coughed and stood. Indeed, he knew exactly. He was having a hard time holding onto his control, so he opted for distance.

"I'm going to refill my wineglass. Would you care for more merlot?"

"No. I'm good." She pointed to her nearly full glass. "No false courage for me."

The remark had him frowning.

Anne waited in the living room. She wasn't sure why she was trying to force Rick's hand, only that after seeing her hand-tinted prints on the wall of his bedroom it suddenly seemed imperative that she know exactly how he felt about her. Maybe it was also because she would be leaving for Japan soon.

Before and after.

She'd never been nervous about the future, but perhaps that had been because it had seemed so clear. Now, it was one big murky mess and, interestingly enough, Rick seemed to be part of the mystery.

When he returned to the living room, she was still on the coffee table in front of his seat. It was almost comical the way he bypassed his chair and walked to the fireplace instead.

"So, you mentioned that J.T. is going with you to Japan," he said as he leaned casually against the mantel.

Anne studied him for a moment before deciding to let him shift the direction of their conversation to a safer topic.

"Yes. My parents offered to come, too, of course, but I told them I thought I should meet Chisato on my own this first time."

"Are you worried that it might be awkward?"

Anne's laughter held no mirth. "For me more so than for them. 'Hello, Chisato. I'm your daughter and this is my mother.' It just seems very weird."

"It's going to be fine—this meeting and any future ones." She appreciated his confidence, even if she didn't appreciate the anticipation in his tone when he asked, "So, have you decided when you will leave?"

"A week from Monday. I figure, why put it off? She's eager to see me and I'm anxious to get this over with."

"Your choice of words is telling, you know," he commented.

"What do you mean?"

"I have no doubt Chisato is *eager* to see you, and, likewise, there's no missing your *anxiety*."

"You know me too well." And he did. Somewhere along the way that fact had stopped bothering her. Instead she found it flattering. Something else did trouble her, though. "I get the feeling I don't know you at all. Why is that?"

"Not much to know."

"Uh-uh." She shook her head for emphasis. "I'm

not buying it. I used to think you were a wading pool, but I'm beginning to realize—"

"That you're in way over your head?" he inserted smoothly. That sardonic smile appeared, along with one raised eyebrow.

"I can swim."

"Better watch out for the undertow."

"Exactly!" She nodded, enjoying the way that he frowned. "A lot goes on under that seemingly placid surface of yours. I get the feeling you have a lot of…secrets."

"Which I intend to keep," he replied. His tone verged on patronizing. It was as if he was trying to push her away. His next question seemed to confirm that theory. "So, any idea how long you will be gone?"

"I don't know. At least a week. I haven't been to Japan in years now, and never to the island where Sapporo is located. I thought I'd take my camera, maybe get some work done while I'm getting to know Chisato and Izumi."

"So, you could be gone longer. Maybe even two weeks or three," he said.

Did he have to appear relieved?

"I guess I could be." Then, before she could think better of it, she asked bluntly, "Are you going to miss me, Rick?"

His pained look did little for her ego. "Anne—"

"Never mind. Don't answer that." She set aside her drink and stood. This was crazy. *She* was crazy. "I'd better be going. It's late."

Rick walked her to the door and then followed her into the chilly night air. His feet were bare, she noted, as her heels clicked along the stone pavers.

"Walking me to my car?" she asked, equal parts amused and touched at the prospect. Even when he was obviously eager to be rid of her, she couldn't fault the man's manners.

"Play your cards right and I'll even open the door for you."

"Ever the gentleman," she teased. Then a little more seriously, she said, "I wonder why it is that some woman hasn't snatched you up already."

"Maybe I'm not as wonderful as I seem," he remarked darkly. Yet he also seemed a little sad.

"Ah. All those secrets you spoke of."

He shrugged. "Actually I prefer bachelorhood. Not everyone is cut out for the marriage-family thing."

His message was not very subtle, but Anne still found it odd. Rick didn't strike her as the type of man who shied away from commitment, and yet any mention of a lasting relationship seemed to have him running and ducking for cover.

At her car, he was as good as his word and held open the door. He stood on the opposite side of it, making it seem almost like a shield. Anne didn't get inside right away, though.

"I feel like I should call you from Japan, let you know how everything goes."

"I'd like that."

"Okay, then. I will." She jingled the keys in her hand. Waiting. Would he kiss her again? After a moment of strained silence, she figured she had her answer. "Well, good night."

"Have a safe trip. I…I want you to be happy, Anne."

"I want you to be happy, too," she told him. In the dim light provided by the moon and her car's dome light, she studied him. "I don't think you are, though. Or that you have been for a long time. I'm right, aren't I, Rick?"

He shook his head. "I'm fine."

"But fine isn't the same as happy," she said quietly.

She reached up to stroke his cheek. It was smooth, leading her to believe he'd shaved in the shower. That seemed like a lot of trouble to go to at this late hour when hc would just have to do it again in the morning. Unless he'd shaved for her benefit. That thought gave her courage.

With the door still between them, Anne rested both of her hands on his shoulders and rose on tiptoe to kiss that smooth cheek. Then she waited a heartbeat and moved a little to the left. This time her lips grazed the corner of his mouth. Even in the dim light, Anne could tell that his eyes were pinched shut. And she could hear his breath begin to chuff in and out.

"What are you doing?"

She chuckled. "You're a bright guy. I think you can figure it out."

"Anne." Her name was but a whisper.

"I find myself needing another—what did you call it the other day?—oh, yeah, gesture of comfort. We can work on happiness after that, maybe even shoot for bliss."

"Anne," he said again.

"Rick," she replied, imitating his frustrated tone. Then she walked around the car door and nudged it closed with her hip. Nothing separated them now. "Why don't you just kiss me?"

In a way, it was goodbye, he told himself. She would be out of the country soon and while she was gone he fully intended to exorcise her from his consciousness. His sanity depended on it. In the meantime, one last kiss couldn't hurt, he reasoned. They were outside, after all, far away from his bed and any other appropriate flat surface. Those pertinent facts filed away, he leaned down and did as she'd requested, managing a little finesse despite his overall restraint.

He should have known Anne would demand more.

She stepped closer, bringing their bodies flush. There was no damp overcoat, no rain slicker to get in the way this time, only a thin layer of clothing that his imagination was already busy removing.

Stop, he ordered himself. End the kiss now and step away. But he didn't. He couldn't. Like an addict he craved more. He wanted and so he took, because this would be it. This kiss would be the end of it, he promised himself, even as the pair of them stumbled together around to the front of her car.

Rick's desperate reaction stole Anne's breath, but what was left of it seemed to catch fire, scorching her lungs as it backed up and burned. His lips were exploring her neck, his fingers alternately clutching and stroking her heated skin. She found herself literally swept off her feet right there in his driveway as he picked her up and then bowed her backward, following her down onto the sloped hood of her car. The metal was still warm from the engine, but it was hard on her back, and it popped in defiance of the added weight. God, what if they left a dent? She'd have a hell of a time explaining the cause to her insurance agent.

Well, she didn't care.

Not now. Not when Rick's mouth was cruising ambitiously down her throat. He tugged the V-neck of her shirt to one side and dropped a kiss on her collarbone. Then his lips moved lower, his hot, ragged breath scorching her skin just above the lacy cup of her demi-bra.

She was about to suggest they return inside when he went still.

"Rick?"

"I'd better stop." He straightened.

"How can you say that?" It came out a near shout. Her body was vibrating with need and he wanted to stop?

"It's not easy," he admitted in a tight voice. "But it's for the best."

She pushed up onto her elbows, making the hood pop again. "Not from where I'm reclining."

"I'm sorry." He shoved a hand through his hair. "God, Anne, we're outside…on your car."

"My back knows exactly where I am, Rick. But I get the feeling that even if we were in your house on something a whole lot more comfortable, you'd be finding a reason to send me on my way." She scooted to the edge of the car so she could sit. Her pride was smarting, but it was the ache in her heart that made her ask, "Why is that?"

He sighed heavily. "It's not you. It's me."

"Yeah, cliché though that may be, I figured as much."

Anne waited for further explanation, but Rick didn't offer any. He tucked his hands into the pockets of his jeans. The gesture made him look younger, vulnerable almost. Secrets, he'd said. Oh, yes, he had lots of them.

When she could stand the silence no longer, she said, "So, are you telling me you just want to be friends?"

She thought he might have grimaced, but he was nodding. "I don't have anything more to offer you."

I think you do. But she kept that thought to herself as she got into her car, fired up the engine and drove away.

CHAPTER NINE

"I HAVE a favor to ask."

A week after Rick last saw Anne, J.T. stood in the doorway to Rick's office, looking uncharacteristically nervous. The last time he'd worn that expression, the Justice Department had been making noise about an antitrust lawsuit.

"What's wrong? Not another call from the Attorney General's office, I hope," Rick said.

"No. Nothing like that." J.T. waved a hand. "It's Marnie. Her blood pressure is up and the doctor wants her to take it easy. He's ordered bed rest for the remainder of her pregnancy."

"But she's okay?" Rick prodded.

"I think so." The beginnings of a smile crinkled J.T.'s blue eyes. "Well, she's pretty cranky about the whole matter, which I'm taking as a good sign. She's making me wait on her hand and foot. Of course, she did that even before the doctor ordered bed rest." His expression turned wry. "She's even got a little silver bell that she rings."

"Really?" Rick did his best to tuck away his smile. "I'm glad she's trying to make the best of a bad situation."

"Oh, she is. Trust me." His boss's expression turned more serious then. "I'll just be relieved when the baby's due-date is here, you know?"

"I'm sure everything's going to be fine," Rick said.

And he prayed that he was right. J.T. and Marnie deserved their happiness. It hadn't come easily to either of them. Something as hard-won as their love surely had to be all the more special, all the more precious because of it.

J.T. wasn't just Rick's employer. He was one of the rare people Rick considered a true friend. He liked the man, and he respected him—enough that Rick had come clean about his not so pleasant past not long after being promoted to his current position. He hadn't wanted anything to shake out later, embarrassing J.T. or proving an embarrassment to Tracker.

J.T. knew all of the secrets Anne had accused Rick of having. Well, except for one. J.T. didn't know Rick was in love with his sister. Friendship or no friendship, he hadn't confided his true feelings on that score. He didn't imagine that one would go over big given everything else J.T. knew about Rick and his tainted pedigree. Besides, what was the point of expressing such feelings when he never intended to act on them?

The kiss from the other night replayed in his head before nipping at his conscience. He wouldn't act on those feelings *again*, Rick amended. He wouldn't see Anne again for a couple of weeks—at least. He'd known that and so he'd given in to the temptation she'd posed at his house the other night. But it wouldn't happen again. No. Never again.

Hardening his resolve, he asked J.T., "So, what's the favor?"

"Well, I don't feel like I can leave Marnie alone right now."

"Of course not," Rick agreed.

"But the thing is, I promised Anne I would go with her to Japan." J.T. scrubbed a hand over the lower half of his face and sighed. "She says she can make the trip alone. You know how stubborn she can be."

"I do indeed." Rick's tone was dry enough to make J.T. smile.

"My folks have offered to go with her, but she doesn't want them to. They aren't sold on the idea of her going by herself, to say the least."

"I can understand that," Rick answered cautiously.

"She doesn't speak the language."

"No."

"And, well, she's a woman, who will be alone in a foreign country, facing a very emotional situation."

"Emotional," Rick repeated and felt his stomach pitch and roll queasily. He had a feeling he knew exactly where this conversation was heading—right into a minefield. Even so, he decided to shelve his own discomfort and forge boldly ahead. Before J.T. could ask properly, Rick offered, "Would you like me to accompany Anne to Japan?"

The smile on J.T.'s face brimmed with relief. "Yes. Thank you, Rick. It's a lot to ask, I know."

"I don't mind," he lied. "I can drop in on the Tokyo office while I'm on that side of the world."

"Oh, you don't need to worry about Tracker business. Looking after Anne while you're there is work enough."

Yes, and didn't Rick know it.

"Speaking of Anne, what does she think about my accompanying her?" Rick inquired, doodling idly in the margin of a legal pad.

J.T. squinted. "Actually she doesn't know. I haven't mentioned it to her yet. I figured I'd better ask you first and make sure you were available."

"I see."

J.T. inhaled deeply then. "On that point I have another favor to ask. Could you not tell her you'll be going?"

Rick's brows rose and he set aside his pen. "You don't want me to tell her I'm going? Your sister tends to be pretty observant, J.T., and the Tracker jet isn't, well, that big. I think she's going to notice I'm on board when it takes off."

A ghost of smile lurked on J.T.'s face. "Yes, but by then it will be too late for her to object."

"I see."

"It's no secret how you two feel about one another."

Rick fought the urge to squirm under the other man's knowing gaze. Good God, was J.T. privy to the fact that Rick had kissed his sister—twice?

"Wh-what do you mean?" he asked casually.

"Just that you two rarely see eye to eye on much of anything."

"No, we don't tend to agree on much," he said slowly.

"And Anne has, in the past, resented your efforts to ensure that the men she becomes involved with aren't gold diggers or corporate spies," J.T. continued.

Rick relaxed slightly. "Yes, she's been pretty vocal on that score, even though I've been right more times than she'd like to admit."

"Well, despite your differences, I'm sure she'll appreciate your company once she has a chance to think about it."

"And a trans-Pacific flight offers nothing if not the time and opportunity for deep thought and reflection," Rick replied.

J.T. grinned. "Exactly."

"Let's hope she sees it that way."

"I'm sure she will. She's grateful for all of your help so far, Rick. In fact, I speak for my parents as well as myself when I say that we all are. You've gone above and beyond the call of duty, but then, you've always been more than an employee to me. More than even a friend." He cleared his throat. "You're like family."

"Thanks." Rick swallowed thickly around the emotions clogging his throat.

"No, thank you." J.T. regarded Rick for a long moment and something in his gaze seemed to add even more weight to the words when he added, "You're a good man and I want you to know that there's *no one* I trust with my sister more than you."

Rick nodded once, guilt swelling right along with his appreciation at such a meaningful compliment. It was the guilt that had him glancing away. He couldn't hold his friend's gaze, not when he knew he didn't deserve such confidence.

Don't trust me.

The words screamed through Rick's head with such force that he marveled they didn't slip past his clenched lips. Somehow, though, he managed to vow, "I won't let you down, J.T."

Now more than ever he was determined to keep that promise.

The door buzzer sounded as Anne straddled the last of her suitcases, trying to mash down her clothes enough so that she could zip the big bag shut. She wasn't having much luck and now her cab had arrived. Thank God she wasn't taking a commercial flight. At least J.T.'s pilot would wait for her no matter how late she arrived at the airport.

She had considered driving her own car instead of calling a cab, but halfway through packing it became clear that her luggage wouldn't fit into her itty-bitty Miata. Half a dozen bags were packed and ready to go. Well, ready to go with the exception of this last stubborn one.

Anne's parents had offered to drive her to the airport, but she had said her goodbyes at their house the evening before and had requested—kindly, but firmly—that they not come to see her off. Anne had to admit, they were being incredibly understanding about the entire matter, especially since J.T. was no longer accompanying her. Anne had been set to postpone her trip when she got word of Marnie's condition, but her parents insisted she go and her sister-in-law would not hear of a delay. In truth, Anne had expected a family "discussion" over the matter—discussion being a code word for argument. But there had been none.

"Marnie isn't scheduled to deliver her baby for a couple of months," her mother had told Anne. "Chisato deserves to see the daughter she delivered three decades ago. That woman has waited long enough."

The intercom buzzed again. Shoving a handful of hair out of her eyes, Anne went to answer it.

"I'll be down in a minute. I'm running a little late."

"Now there's a surprise," a familiar voice replied blandly through the speaker.

Anne fumbled for the button again. "Rick? Is that you?"

"You got it in one."

"What are you doing down there?"

"I've come for you."

His simply worded statement raised gooseflesh on Anne's arms and had her heart knocking out an extra beat before she realized that what he meant was he had come to take her to the airport.

"Did J.T. ask you to do this?"

He seemed to hesitate. Then, "Yes."

She struggled not to be disappointed with his answer.

"Come on up. I could use a hand with my luggage," she told him through the intercom before depressing the button that unlocked the door downstairs.

Anne waited at the top of the steps, smiling awkwardly when Rick passed the first landing and came into view. She hadn't spoken to him since he'd kissed her horizontal in his driveway, even though she'd hoped he would call. The fact that he hadn't still rankled. Okay, it more than rankled. It hurt. Every time she thought she had broken through his dense wall of restraint, he quickly erected another barrier.

"This is a surprise." She twisted her hands together. The stones in her collection of jade, quartz and lapis bracelets tinkled like wind chimes and tattled on her nerves. She tucked her hands into the back pockets of her jeans and worked up a smile.

"I probably should have called to let you know I was coming."

She shrugged. "That's okay. It's…it's just that I didn't think I would be seeing you again. Before I left for Japan, I mean. And after…" She coughed.

Rick said nothing as he joined her in the doorway, although his brows rose. His silence seemed to dare Anne to go on. She didn't, though, and neither did he. Not that staying mum on the matter did much good. That lock of lips seemed to hang in the air between them, as conspicuous as a treat-filled piñata. As the silence stretched, Anne wondered who would be brave enough—or foolish enough—to take a whack at it first.

"You said you needed help with your bags," he said at last.

Chicken, she almost said aloud, but then she was nodding.

"Oh. Yes. Right. In here." The response came out staccato. Apparently she was no braver.

He followed Anne into her room. She was pleased

that at least this time the space was orderly. No garments, let alone unmentionables, were heaped on the floor, and the bed was neatly made, half a dozen fat pillows stacked in front of the carved wood of its headboard.

Lined up near its foot were five bags of varying shapes and sizes. The sixth one sat half open on the floor, bits of colorful fabric spitting out its sides like the tongues of defiant children.

"Can you give me a hand?" Anne asked, kneeling atop it and trying to shove cotton and silk away from the zipper.

Rick surveyed the assortment of luggage with a scowl pinching his features. "Jeez, Anne, how long do you plan to be gone? It looks like you're moving to Japan."

"I just packed the essentials," she replied tightly.

"Yes, but for how many people?"

She glanced at the bags. Okay, she had gone overboard, but in addition to the bag containing her camera equipment, one entire suitcase was dedicated to shoes and jewelry. Men just didn't understand such things. For them, one pair of wing tips and a nice watch could cover nearly everything in their wardrobe. Women didn't get that lucky. Besides, Anne wasn't sure what she would need in Japan. Casual? Dressy? A combination of the two? It had seemed a smart bet to pack half the contents of her closet.

"It's not a commercial flight. I can bring whatever I like," she informed him, kneeling on the bag and yanking at the zipper.

"There's a weight limit on Tracker's jet, too, you know. But maybe the co-pilot can stay behind."

"Smart a—"

"Ah-ah-ah," Rick interrupted with a wag of his finger. "Is that any way to talk to the cavalry?"

With that he lowered one knee onto the suitcase next to hers. The added weight forced the two sides of the big bag together. Of course, zipping it took some interesting maneuvering since Anne had to reach around Rick's solid build to finish the job. If the fact that her cheek brushed against his chest bothered him, though, he didn't let it show. He seemed oddly detached, almost as if that encounter—*either* encounter, for that matter—had never taken place.

And men had the nerve to say women were baffling. She couldn't figure him out. One minute, she was sure he was as interested and attracted as she was. The next he seemed to have stepped so far back she needed binoculars just to read his expression.

With one last tug, the zipper reached the end of its run. Turning so she could sit on the bag, Anne said, "Thanks."

"No problem."

He sat on the bag as well then, elbows resting on his bent knees. He was wearing his usual corporate attire. She was picturing him in a sweaty T-shirt and shorts.

"Out of curiosity," he asked, adjusting his cuff links. "How exactly were you planning to get this thing down the steps without killing yourself?"

"Let's just say my cabdriver was going to earn a really, really big tip."

"Enough to pay for his hernia surgery?" Rick asked, that single eyebrow winging skyward.

"I guess I won't find out now that you're here." She smiled. "Good thing Tracker provides excellent health care benefits."

The intercom buzzer sounded then.

"Speak of the devil," Anne said. "Looks like my cab has arrived."

"I'll let the driver know you no longer require his services." Rick rose and motioned around the room. "Finish up whatever you need to finish up. I'll be right back."

Even with their wheels and retractable handles, Anne's luggage proved formidable to move. It took her and Rick two trips each, but they finally managed to get all of the bags down to the curb where a car waited. It wasn't Rick's sporty, red two-seater. Anne thanked God for that since it would have accommodated no more of her luggage than her own small Miata would have. No, this was a sleek limousine, no doubt courtesy of Tracker Operating Systems. The black-capped driver hopped out to help them with the bags.

"J.T.'s awfully thoughtful," Anne remarked, handing over the last of her suitcases.

"Actually the limo was my idea." Just when she was feeling all warm and fuzzy over his thoughtfulness, he shrugged. "I figured you'd overpack."

"I didn't overpack," she insisted, settling onto the rich leather upholstery with a sigh while the driver hefted her bags into the vehicle's ample trunk. "I merely planned for every eventuality."

"That's also known as overpacking," Rick informed her dryly, taking the seat opposite hers.

Then they were leaving. The retort Anne planned died on her lips. Her breath hitched as she glanced over her shoulder and watched the Victorian that housed her apartment shrink in the rear window. Before and after, she thought again. When she faced forward, Rick was watching her intently. He seemed to read her mind.

"Things have changed, but you're going to be fine," he said quietly.

"I hope you're right."

Anne had been on J.T.'s corporate jet often enough to know where he kept the good stuff, so she filched a cinnamon-dusted truffle from the gold box of chocolates hidden away in the small galley and returned to her seat.

The jet, a sleek number that could accommodate a dozen passengers in the lap of luxury, would be taking off in a matter of minutes. The chocolate was for courage. In general, Anne didn't have a problem with flying. Not only was it the quickest way to get from Point A to Point B, she also liked the idea of defying gravity and soaring through the clouds. No, it wasn't flying that she minded. It was her destination as well as the overall reason behind her trip that had her nerves frayed this time. Add Rick to her emotional quagmire and was it any wonder that a box of calorie-laden chocolates was calling her name?

She'd thought maybe he would kiss her again, especially since he'd surprised her by escorting her up the steps and into the jet's cabin as the limo driver and ground crew saw to her luggage. The gesture was sweet, but then Anne reminded herself that J.T. had asked Rick to see her off, and on the way to the airport, their conversation had never veered away from polite small talk. The man who had pressed her back onto the hood of her car in his eagerness and urgency was nowhere to be found.

Once inside the jet, Rick had ducked into the cockpit, apparently to have a word with the pilot, and Anne had decided to find a seat in the spacious cabin and make herself comfortable.

Now, truffle in hand, she snuggled into a wide leather chair, pulled the seat belt tight across her hips and popped the confection into her mouth whole. She pulled out her iPod, plugged in the earphones and, closing her eyes, let Billie Holiday's inspired vocals and a few hundred calories of Godiva's finest soothe her soul right along with her wounded ego.

"Lady Day" was caressing the notes of a third song when the jet's engines revved to life. Anne started, unable to believe that Rick hadn't said goodbye. She opened her eyes, and then blinked in surprise. The man in question was in the seat that faced hers. He'd shed his suit coat, which was carefully laid over one of the seats on the opposite side of the aisle, and he was reading a business journal. He was the picture of professional sophistication and way too relaxed for her liking.

"Wh-what are you doing?" she asked, tugging out the earphones. "My God, Rick, the pilot is gearing up for takeoff. We're going to be in the air in a matter of minutes."

He looked up. "Oh, right."

But instead of jumping out of his seat and bolting for the exit, he casually lifted the end of his safety belt and secured it across his lap.

"Rick!" she hollered, incredulous.

One side of his mouth lifted then. "Oh, didn't I mention that I'm coming, too?"

"Y-y-you're coming with me to Japan?" Anne sputtered.

"Yes."

She didn't care for his high-handed approach. No, not one bit. He might have told her. He might have *asked* if she'd appreciate his tagging along. Even so, she found herself smiling in return.

"Thanks. This means a lot to me."

"Yes, well, favor to J.T." His clipped response had her smile faltering.

"Is that the only reason?" she wanted to ask. She wanted to shout the words that were perched on her tongue, but she swallowed them whole. Pride had her replying instead, "Whatever the reason, I'm glad for the company."

She slipped the earphones back in then, closed her eyes and, even as her heart ached, she was determined to do her best to ignore him for the remainder of the long trip. Less easy to ignore, however, were her feelings.

Her personal life seemed to be in chaos. Everything she knew and had understood about her past was being challenged and uprooted. And here she was falling in love.

Barely a month earlier Anne hadn't figured the pair of them had much of anything in common. She'd considered Rick an acquaintance as well as an occasional annoyance. She'd never looked beyond his controlled mannerisms and aloof exterior to the man beneath. Then she'd gone to him for help, knowing instinctively that she could trust him and that he wouldn't let her down.

The physical attraction she felt had come as a surprise, and not an unwelcome one. Anne had been too intrigued by it to try to deny its existence. But attraction wasn't what had her heart wobbling on a high ledge now. No, it was what she had discovered about Rick during these past few weeks. She'd always known he was smart and his sense of humor dry. But he was thoughtful, too, kind, insightful, a good listener and an even better friend. He made attributes like dependability and stability sexy and enticing. And he made Anne want to erase the pain of his past or whatever it was that caused him to try so hard to camouflage his true self from her view.

Tell me your secrets, she wanted to beg. But she knew he wasn't ready. The scarier prospect was that he might never be.

The jet finally reached cruising altitude and Anne was dying for another truffle. Just when it seemed safe to unbuckle her seat belt, though, turbulence had the cabin bucking like a carnival ride.

"Better keep that thing fastened," Rick said when the rough patch of air continued. Over the top of the magazine, gray-green eyes regarded Anne intently. "Looks like it could be bumpy for a while yet."

"Tell me about it," she murmured.

CHAPTER TEN

ANNE slept through the jet's arrival on Hokkaido. Just as well, Rick thought, watching her. There were shadows beneath her eyes, and even in repose, her brow was furrowed from worry.

He hadn't wanted to come to Japan with her. He'd told himself that with Anne out of sight he somehow would be able to put her out of his mind. Well, he'd lied to himself then, just as he'd lied to her when he'd told her that the only reason he'd come to Sapporo was that J.T. had asked him to. The truth was, no matter what this cost him personally, Rick wanted to be here with her at this important crossroads in her life.

He left his seat, giving in to the urge to touch her while she slept, and crouched down in front of her. God, she was lovely, even in her exhaustion. Her head was tilted to one side and so he pushed the dark curtain of hair back from her cheek to tuck it behind her ear. Ignoring all of his head's sound arguments to the contrary, he dropped a light kiss onto her lips.

Anne's long eyelids fluttered momentarily and Rick used the opportunity to rise to his feet before she managed to focus. When she smiled up at him, he thought his knees would give out.

"We're here," he managed to say.

She nodded, straightened. Her smile turned slightly apprehensive, but her resolve was unmistakable when she told him, "I'm ready."

For the next couple of days Anne rested up from the long flight and took in the sights around Sapporo. Gidayu had been at the airport to greet them when they arrived. He'd smiled warmly at her, handing her a huge bouquet of lilies courtesy of Chisato and Izumi. His expression had held an odd bit of challenge when he'd bowed to Rick.

"I did not realize you would be here."

"Change of plans."

"Mine are the same," Gid had said cryptically and then he'd turned to Anne. "Your mother and sister thought it best for you to get your bearings before you meet."

Anne was grateful they had not delivered the flowers in person. After the long flight, and given her own high emotions, the last thing she had wanted to experience was an awkward scene in some airport. Part of her was eager to have the initial meeting with her biological family over with and out of the way. But another part of her was perfectly happy to postpone the inevitable and play tourist for a couple of days with Rick, even if he was once again acting distant and annoyingly polite.

She swore the man must have memorized a guide book or two, because even though he claimed never to have been to Sapporo, he had no problem squiring Anne around. And, of course, he was full of interesting tidbits of information, explaining how the island of Hokkaido had remained largely unsettled by the Japanese until the later part of the 1800s. Before that, it had been called Ezo and populated mainly by the indigenous Ainu people.

Anne took her camera with her on their outings, finding it easier to be an observer in this land of her ancestors as the time ticked down to her meeting with Chisato. Behind the viewfinder of her Nikon, she could lose herself to the scenery. Her artist's eye liked what she saw, especially the many contrasts, both natural and man-made.

Beyond Sapporo's modern skyline, mountains rose up, majestic and timeless. The city, Japan's fifth-largest with nearly two million residents, was amazingly Western in many regards. Even her hotel room had all of the amenities one would expect from a five-star establishment back in the States. Yet Sapporo was uniquely Japanese in other ways and exuded a kind of charm Anne found surprising for a city so large. It also was amazingly safe and clean. Statistically, violent crime was all but unheard of and even its subway trains were unmarred by graffiti.

She and Rick took the public transportation system to most places, leaving their rental car at the hotel. Anne enjoyed being among the people. She couldn't speak the language, although she was interested now in learning it and Rick was proving to be a patient teacher. She didn't quite fit in here, but neither was she the anomaly she'd been growing up as one of the few Asian students in her suburban Iowa school district.

On the afternoon of their third day in Sapporo, they walked from their hotel to nearby Nakajima Park, where Rick surprised her by renting a rowboat to take out onto Shobu Pond. The gesture was romantic, even though he let go of her hand immediately after helping her into the boat.

Anne picked up her camera, snapping off a dozen shots of the lush scenery before turning the lens on Rick.

"Just documenting my journey," she said when his brows rose in question.

"Then why take my picture?"

She lowered the camera, cradled it in her lap. "You seem to be part of it."

She lifted the camera again and managed several shots as he regarded her quietly, and when she viewed them on the camera's display afterward, she swore she glimpsed emotions that were deeper and stronger than those to which he was apparently willing to own up.

She considered confronting him about the matter, but then the invitation for lunch at Chisato's home came when they arrived back at the hotel. She'd expected it, of course, based on the conversations she'd had with Gid at the airport and since her arrival. Even so, the politely worded missive had apprehension growing right along with the lump in her throat.

What was she going to say to her birth mother? Or to her younger half sister, for that matter? What if the three of them stared blankly at one another after the initial introductions and exchanges of information were made? What if Anne felt no connection to them at all?

What if she felt too much of one?

"You're coming with me, right?" she asked that evening as Rick sat across the dinner table from her, expertly eating ramen noodles with his chopsticks. Anne had given up long ago and ordered a hamburger.

"Of course. Stop worrying," he said mildly.

"Who says I'm worrying?"

He merely gave her a bland look before taking a sip of his green tea. "Tomorrow will take care of itself, Anne."

"Yeah, right."

"It will," he insisted.

She set aside her burger and wiped her hands on a paper napkin. "You know, that's interesting advice coming from you."

"Why?"

"Because you don't follow it."

Rick said nothing, but Anne knew she'd touched a nerve because the noodles that had been on his chopsticks were now sliding down his shirtfront.

The neighborhood where Chisato lived was populated with wood-framed homes with tidy, tiny yards. The houses were relatively small compared to the American ones Anne was used to, but the Japanese, even those making a comfortable living, didn't go for the kinds of big, showy places that were common in California's affluent neighborhoods.

As Anne stood at the door, Rick brushed his fingers across her cheek. The touch was friendly, as was his smile. It still caused her pulse to pick up speed.

"Ready?" he asked, raising that same hand to knock. She nodded.

Gidayu answered almost immediately, smiling warmly and bowing in welcome.

"Hello, Anne. It is a pleasure to see you again. And Mr. Danton, too, of course."

"I'm sure," Rick grunted half under his breath.

"It's good to see you, Gid," Anne said. "I'm afraid I was a bit drained when we met at the airport."

"Understandable after such a long flight. I trust you are well-rested now?"

"Yes."

"Good. Your mother and sister are most happy to finally meet you. And a little nervous, too, I think. They are…composing themselves and will join us shortly."

"I know the feeling," Anne replied, working up a smile. She worried her hands together, making the beads of her bracelets clink and tinkle as the three of them stepped into the entryway, which Anne remembered Rick had referred to as the *genkan*.

Rick put a hand on her shoulder. Leaning down, he whispered. "Relax." His grip intensified when she started forward into the house. "Shoes," he said quietly.

"Oh, right."

She slipped her feet out of the smart heels she'd selected to go with the slim fitting skirt and collared silk blouse. She'd gone through five outfits before settling on this one, which she thought of as Sunday brunch casual. God, but she hadn't felt this uncertain over her appearance since the ninth grade, when one of the most popular boys in her school had asked her to the spring formal. She'd changed her mind on a gown half a dozen times before her mother had finally put her foot down and refused to take Anne back to the shopping mall.

Her mother.

"Come this way," Gidayu was saying.

It was galling, but Rick had to actually nudge her along. Anne felt rooted in place, chained to the spot just inside the door as a kaleidoscope of emotions tumbled and swirled.

They turned a corner and then stepped through a sliding, paper-lined door into a sparsely furnished room that had woven mats on the floor. The texture was pure bliss on her bare feet.

"Nice," she murmured, glancing at Rick in question.

"Tatami," he whispered back.

The sitting room was sparsely decorated in the traditional Japanese way. The exception was the alcove, or *tokonoma,* whose staggered shelves Anne knew held the family's treasured belongings. Something familiar caught her eye and she walked over for a closer look. On one of the shelves was an eight-by-ten framed hand-tinted print. It bore Anne's signature in the bottom right-hand corner.

"She owns some of my work," Anne said, surprised, honored.

"Yes," Gid replied. "She purchased it on eBay several months ago."

Anne frowned in confusion. "But several months ago she didn't know for certain I was her daughter."

"She knew, Ayano," he said simply. "That is why it was so important for her to have something that your hands had once touched. It was a way she could be close to you."

The stirring explanation had Anne's gaze veering to Rick. Her heart picked up speed, bucking against her ribs in time with the blood that had begun to roar in her ears.

Despite those two rather erotic encounters, he'd done his damnedest to keep her at arm's length. He had secrets, ones that kept him from making commitments. But what if…what if…?

"Is that the reason?" she asked, her tone verging on a demand.

"Of course." Gid sounded a little offended by the question. He did not realize Anne hadn't directed it at him.

"Rick?"

He owned her artwork, too. In fact, he owned what Anne considered to be four of her most emotion-laden prints. Lovers. Their clasped hands, their wrapped arms. He didn't know that she knew that, though, and so she held her breath, waiting for his reply and wondering what it might reveal.

He nodded slowly. And when he spoke, his answer lifted her heart at the same time that it broke it.

"She loves you, Anne. Your art is a way to be close to you, as Gid says. It's the only part of you that she's been able to have. That's not so hard to understand, is it?"

Her eyes filled, but Anne was smiling. No. Not so hard to understand at all. "Rick, I—"

But before she could continue, Gid was clearing his

throat and gesturing with his hand. Not the right place, not the right time, Anne reminded herself as the paper-lined door on the opposite side of the room slid open and the moment she had alternately dreaded and antic-ipated for weeks finally arrived.

An older Japanese woman stepped into the room, followed by another woman who was much closer to Anne's age. But it was Chisato who nabbed her atten-tion, whose overly bright gaze had Anne holding her breath.

The woman was in her mid-fifties and yet Anne's first impression was that time had been exceedingly kind. Other than the fine lines that fanned out from her eyes and a few random streaks of gray in her dark, neatly coiffed chin-length hair, the older woman exuded vitality and health.

And strength. Even now, with unshed tears making her eyes swim, Chisato remained composed enough to smile politely and bow.

"Ayano," she whispered. She reached for Anne's hand and said something in Japanese before apparently repeating it in halting English. "My little daughter is not so little now. She is beautiful young woman."

Anne hadn't been sure what emotion she would ex-perience when she came face-to-face with the person who had given her life. Even now she wasn't sure what she was feeling, but knew that certain questions were answered. Questions that she hadn't even realized had nagged at her until exactly this moment.

Oh, she'd always known that her distinctly Asian features had come from her birth mother. But it went beyond that. She'd met plenty of people back in San Francisco with similarly shaped eyes and rounded faces. She'd never looked at them and felt this kind of recognition. It was as if she had finally discovered the last piece to a puzzle and, by inserting it, the entire picture had become clear.

Anne stared at the older woman and saw herself.

Chisato had the same nose—small and slightly flared at the nostrils—as Anne's. Her mouth was shaped the same, too, although Anne's lips were fuller and a little wider. And they shared that same stubborn cowlick just to the right of their parts. They were similar in build, too, about the same height now that Anne had shed her high heels. Chisato's posture was straight, her clothing surprisingly Western and the necklace looped around her neck was something Anne would have picked out for herself.

Anne's gaze turned to Izumi then. The younger woman was slighter in build than Anne was. Her face was rounder and her eyes spaced farther apart. Izumi smiled hesitantly, bowed and then offered a hand.

"I am Izumi," she said, the introduction unnecessary and yet all the more endearing for it.

"Yes. *Imooto,*" Anne said, using the word Rick had taught her for younger sister. Her gaze returned to Chisato. *"Okaa-san,"* she said. It was not a betrayal to Jeanne Lundy at all, she realized, to call this other woman Mother.

"I have waited so long for this day," Chisato replied, a tear slipping down her cheek. "So many, many years. I not give up hope. A mother cannot give up hope. And now you are here." The tears flowed in earnest then. "My Ayano, home at last."

Anne's own emotions spilled over as well. Home? No, this would never be home. Home would always be wherever Jeanne and Ike Lundy lived. But this place, these women, they were undeniably special, too. Her overtaxed brain tried to figure out how it would all work out in the end, but she couldn't manage it. Indeed, she couldn't seem to think at all. She could only feel as the two distinct sides of her life—sides that had never so much as bumped, let alone overlapped—suddenly collided and merged.

For the next couple of hours, as Anne sat on a futon next to Rick and traded information with Chisato and Izumi, she experienced a completion she hadn't expected or even realized she'd been seeking.

Since arriving in Japan, she'd been waiting for a sign, something big and irrefutable that would tell her that she had ended up where she should have been, in the right family and with the right mother. It wasn't as simple as that, though, she realized now. But neither was it as complicated as Anne had made it. She had *two* mothers. Two women who loved her equally and had played different roles in her life. Jeanne had said as much, of course. Anne just hadn't been ready to listen or to understand.

Now she was.

Through it all, Rick stayed at her side, his hand clasping hers in a way that reminded Anne of the photographs she'd taken and then tinted. Photographs that Rick owned. Not so long ago, he had assured her that what happened in the days ahead was up to her. He'd claimed she was in charge, in control. Well, now she knew exactly what—and who—she wanted her future to include.

Anne was quiet on the drive back from Chisato's home. Rick didn't take offense. She was certainly entitled to her introspection given the day she'd had. Every now and then, though, from the corner of his eye, he would catch her watching him. She didn't say a word, though. Not until he'd handed off the rental car's keys to the valet and ushered her inside the hotel's main lobby.

"Would you join me for a drink, please?"

"A drink?" He blinked. "I figured you'd want to call home, talk to J.T. or your folks."

"I do. Eventually. Right now, I want to talk to you."

"Everything okay, Anne?"

"Fine. Never better, in fact."

"Okay," he said slowly, not quite trusting that bright smile of hers. "Do you want to go out someplace or will one of the hotel lounges do?"

"Actually I was thinking more like a hotel *suite.*"

"A suite?" His molars clicked together.

"Yes. Mine or yours? We both have fully stocked mini-bars that are just begging to be raided." She smiled again. "Besides, I'd appreciate the privacy."

"You want privacy?" Oh, this couldn't be good.

"Yes. There are some things—observations, I guess you could call them—that I've made, and I'd really like your opinion on them."

Rick swallowed. What she was telling him was that she needed an adviser, a sounding board. That was part of the reason J.T. had asked Rick to accompany her to Japan. How could he say no? The short answer was he couldn't.

"Your suite," he said. At least that left him the option of leaving. "I'm happy to help."

The moment they stepped across the threshold to her rooms, though, he was not quite so happy. No, what he was when Anne sighed heavily and slipped off her shoes, was turned on.

And that was before she said, "I'm just going to change into something a little more comfortable."

"Comfortable," he repeated.

"Yeah. Why don't you loosen that tie of yours, take off your jacket and help yourself to whatever looks good in the mini-bar. Get the same for me."

Rick scrubbed a hand over his face once she'd disappeared inside the bedroom and willed the blood back up to his brain. He could do this, he told himself. He could be her friend. He selected a couple of small bottles of chilled sake from the mini-bar and then dialed room service. Anne had hardly eaten anything all day, and so he ordered two cheeseburgers with fries for their entrée and *mochi,* a traditional egg custard, for dessert. He figured it was as good a blend of east and west as could be mustered at the moment. Besides, that ensured they would have at least one interruption within the next hour.

Fifteen minutes later the door leading to the bedroom opened and Anne emerged. She'd pulled her long hair into a ponytail and had changed into low-slung jeans and a button-down blouse whose hem played peekaboo with her navel.

Rick reached for his sake.

She eyed him for a moment. "You're still wearing your jacket, Rick. You haven't even loosened your tie."

"I'm fine."

"Well, you don't look relaxed."

"I'm fine," he repeated.

She merely raised her eyebrows and so he stood and shrugged out of the jacket. "There."

"Tie?"

He loosened it a mere inch, his expression just this side of patronizing. "Satisfied?"

"Are you kidding?" She laughed outright, the sound smugly female.

Time to change the subject, he decided. "I, um, ordered dinner from room service. You didn't eat much at Chisato's house. I figured you shouldn't drink on an empty stomach."

"You're always looking out for me."

"Yes." He cleared his throat, but his voice remained unnaturally strained when he added, "Our food should be here any time."

"Okay. I guess I am hungry." She dropped onto the opposite side of the couch and pulled her bare feet up underneath her, watching him.

"You mentioned earlier that you wanted my opinion." One side of his mouth rose. "You know, another time, another place I'd have to rub that in."

"Well, then, I appreciate your restraint."

He smiled fully now, finding his footing for a brief moment before she pulled the rug out from under him again. "You exercise a lot of restraint when it comes to me, don't you, Rick?"

"Sorry?" He bluffed, pretending he didn't understand exactly what she meant.

Anne waved a hand. Beads tinkled before she removed her bracelets and set them on the low table in front of them. The move seemed like a challenge, especially when she unbuttoned the cuffs on her shirt and rolled up her sleeves. Then she stood and walked to a large piece of modern art that hung on the far wall.

"I was really touched that Chisato owns some of my work," she remarked, running a finger along the bottom edge of the picture's chrome frame.

The topic was safer, but the swift switch in subject made him oddly nervous.

"It's a nice piece. Part of your waterfront collection, I believe."

"It's interesting that you seem to know so much about my work and yet you don't own any of it." She turned, brows raised.

"I… Um…"

She walked toward him, her dark gaze as single-minded and intense as that of a panther on the prowl.

"What was it you said earlier, Rick, in explaining why Chisato would own my art?"

He cleared his throat. "I think I mentioned that owning something you'd created would be, um, important to her."

"Why?"

"Well, it's the only part of you she's been able to have."

"Yes, and what other reason did you give?"

His voice came out an appalling whisper. "Because she loves you."

"Ah." She smiled, looking both triumphant and touched. "I remember now." She took the glass of sake from his hand, sipped from it. He watched her lips close over the ceramic rim and licked his own. "Do you own any of my work?" she asked point-blank.

"Well, I…" His voice trailed off pitifully. God, he hadn't seen any of this coming. He needed to redirect the conversation and quickly. Sarcasm, he thought. That always helped provide distance.

But before he could speak Anne said, "Let's just skip to the chase, shall we? I know that you do. Four pieces, my lovers' series, to be exact. And they're on your bedroom wall."

"You were in my bedroom?" He mustered up outrage, hoping that would put her off.

She merely shrugged. "What can I say? Curiosity got the better of me and so I peeked."

"I fail to see what that has to do with—"

But he didn't get out the rest of the words before she set aside the glass of sake, leaned over and plucked up his tie. She wound the pricey silk around her hand, reeling him toward her like a damned bass on a fishing line.

"How are your toes feeling? Let me know when they curl," she had the nerve to say before straddling his lap and kissing him full on the mouth.

Control snapped. Or maybe he'd never had it in the first place when it came to this woman, he admitted. Well, he wanted some now…a different kind of control. He shifted their positions until Anne was beneath him, his full weight melting into her gentle curves and pressing her down into the couch cushions.

"Anne," he moaned as her small hands tugged the shirt from his trousers and then snaked up his back, nails raking his flesh with the same eager anticipation he felt. "We're wearing too many damned clothes."

"My thought exactly," she replied, bringing her hands around so she could unbutton his shirt and then she was shoving it down his arms. A moment later her blouse joined his in the heap on the floor.

"You're perfect," he said.

"I'm going to remind you that you said that." Her laughter was a little breathless because his fingers were stroking the flesh that swelled above the satin bra she wore.

"I'll plead insanity." His lips followed the trail of his fingertips.

"Oh, no. This moment isn't about insanity. Or even sex for that matter. You love me. Say it," she demanded, pushing on his shoulders until he leaned back far enough to see her face. "Right now, Rick, please tell me the truth."

Her simple plea breached his defenses. The floodgates opened and his closely guarded emotions spilled out in a raging torrent.

"I love you, Anne. I've loved you nearly as long as I've known you. God help me, I'll love you till the day I die."

She was grinning when she pulled him down for another kiss. Just as his hand struggled with the clasp at the front of her bra, a knock sounded at the door. Even as

Rick breathed heavily and tried to subdue his pulse, he knew that reality had arrived right along with room service.

The young man who delivered their meal wheeled it in on a linen-covered cart, bowed politely and handed Anne a slip of paper to sign. As soon as he was gone she turned to find Rick not only with his shirt on, but wearing his suit coat and adjusting his tie.

"Are you leaving?" she asked, incredulous.

"I think that would be for the best."

"Oh? See, I reached a different conclusion when you were unbuttoning my blouse a minute ago. Care to tell me how you came to yours?" she asked sharply, her patience waning, even as her body's reaction to him was still humming along on high.

"Anne, look, what just happened between us isn't a good idea."

"Why? I love you, too, Rick."

She expected the words to garner a reaction and they did. He blinked, almost as if he couldn't believe his good fortune, but then he was frowning again.

"It's still not a good idea," he replied, looking so distant and sounding so damned controlled. Not now, she thought. She would have none of that now.

"I just told you that I love you and I know you love me. In fact, if memory serves me right, you mentioned that your feelings for me were hardly a recent development."

"They aren't."

"So, how is our being together *not* a good idea?"

"Well, first of all, you're J.T.'s sister."

That rationale ticked her off but good. "My brother has nothing to do with this and you know it. Besides, he likes and respects you, Rick. If I called him right now and told him about us, he'd be nothing but pleased."

He was shaking his head, though. "I don't think so, Anne. He likes me and he respects me, but that's not the same as thinking I'm good enough for his sister."

Rick had never struck her as the type of man with an inferiority complex, yet she didn't doubt he believed what he was saying. For the first time, Anne found herself wishing for an appearance of his cocky confidence that she'd found so infuriating in the past.

"What are you talking about?"

"There's no *us*, Anne."

"Why?" she asked again, pushing back the pain his words caused. She wasn't being a glutton for punishment. She would walk away if she had to, but she needed to know the reason she was leaving.

"I'm not…right for you."

"Oh, I don't know, you seemed pretty right for me just now on the couch."

"That was an impulsive and not very smart thing to do," he had the nerve to say.

"No, *that* was a long time coming and we both know it. But for room service's untimely interruption, we'd both be naked and sweaty right now." When she saw his Adam's apple bob, she added, "And well on our way to mutual satisfaction for what undoubtedly would be the first time of many this evening."

"God, would you stop!"

"I'm just stating facts. Being a lawyer, I thought you would appreciate facts."

"I'd appreciate it if you'd just accept what I'm saying and leave it at that."

"Give me reasons, *real* reasons, and maybe I will. Why won't you give us a chance? What are you so afraid of?" she demanded quietly.

"Let's talk about this another time," he began. "You're upset. It's been an emotional day, meeting Chisato and Izumi, and all."

"I'm upset, all right, but please don't belittle what's going on between us by pretending it was a reaction to stress. You tried that once before, remember? I didn't buy it then. I don't now."

He rubbed his eyes, but remained stubbornly silent.

"Don't I get to decide who is right for me?"

"Not in this instance, Anne. I'm sorry."

He started for the door, but she blocked his exit.

"Of all the high-handed, bullheaded…" She huffed out a deep breath. "I can't believe you're still trying to run my love life."

"Someone has to watch out for you."

She'd thought she was angry before.

"Yes, because I attract such losers, as you've so kindly pointed out on more than one occasion in the past." Crossing her arms over her chest, she demanded, "So, Rick, tell me, what's wrong with you? I know you're not after a job at Tracker. You already have one. And you're not after a chunk of my brother's fortune. You're too proud and independent to ever sponge off someone else. Besides, you do well enough financially on your own. So, what's your deficiency?"

When he said nothing, Anne steamrolled ahead.

"Come on, Rick, tell me the deep, dark secret that you somehow feel makes you unworthy of dating the illustrious J.T. Lundy's baby sister or having a serious, committed relationship with any woman, for that matter?"

"I'm leaving now."

He reached for the handle, but she refused to budge, even when the door thumped against her back.

"Move, Anne. Please."

She almost relented. He sounded so miserable. But she shook her head. She was miserable, too. And misery loved company.

"Tell me your secrets first. Let me judge for myself."

"Fine," he said at last, spitting out the word. "You want to know my deep, dark secrets?"

"Yes."

"Be sure, Anne. Be damned sure," he warned.

His tone was so dire she almost lost her nerve. But she nodded. "I'm sure. I love you."

"Then you love a monster."

She frowned and shook her head in confusion.

"I killed my father, Anne. I killed my own father. Is that the kind of man you want to love?"

His words shocked her, but no more so than the utter despondency that drenched his tone. He was staring at his hands, at the fists that were now clenched and shaking.

"I was fourteen years old. Fourteen! And I don't regret doing it. Do you understand what I'm saying,

Anne? Do you get it? I'd do it again, if I had to. Even knowing what it makes me, I'd still stop him."

When he reached past her for the door handle this time, she stepped out of the way. She let him leave, because she wasn't sure what to say to stop him.

CHAPTER ELEVEN

ANNE might have been confused about a lot of things when Rick stormed out, but on one point she was certain: The man was no murderer. J.T. further clarified the issue when she called him a few minutes later.

"Anne, good to hear from you, even if I was hoping to sleep in this morning," he said on a yawn.

"Sorry. Just needed to talk."

"How did it go today?" he asked, sounding only a little bleary from the time difference.

Anne told him about meeting Chisato and Izumi. Emotionally she felt as if she were on a roller coaster. For the past few weeks, she'd shot down one perilously steep hill after another. She'd thought she was done, the long, crazy ride over at last. She'd reconnected with her birth family and she'd finally gotten Rick to admit his true feelings for her. And yet here she was atop another rise and poised to plunge into the abyss again.

"Actually, J.T., the reason I'm calling right now isn't just to talk about my birth family. There's...another matter I need to discuss with you."

"Oh? What's up?"

"Well, it involves Rick."

She swore there was a grin in her brother's voice when he said, "You two getting along okay?"

"Fine." She fiddled with the buttons on her blouse, remembering how Rick had so deftly unfastened them less than an hour before. "We're getting along better than fine, actually."

She shifted in her seat on the couch, squirming a bit during the long pause that ensued. Finally she asked, "Are you there?"

"Yeah, sorry." Her brother's deep laughter rumbled. "So, is that a discreet euphemism for what I think it is?"

"Yes."

"You sound…very serious."

"I feel very serious. I…I love him."

"Gee, Anne, could you provide a scorecard or something? It's hard to keep up with all of the major developments in your life."

"Tell me about it." She paused. "J.T., you don't have a problem with me seeing Rick, do you?"

"No. None."

"He seems to think you would."

"Do you want me to talk to him, clear the air?"

"Yes…no." She sighed. "It's more than that, J.T."

"What's wrong, Anne?"

She told him about Rick's startling revelation, holding her breath afterward, but she needn't have bothered.

"It was self-defense. Pure and simple."

"You knew?"

"Sure. Rick told me about it long ago and I looked

into it for myself. His father was an abusive SOB, not only to Rick but to his mother. Rick finally got big enough to fight back and he did. The court ruled the death self-defense. Unfortunately, his mother never forgave him. Apparently she loved the guy, warts and all. Rick ended up in foster care until his eighteenth birthday."

"Oh, my God."

"Yeah, well, good thing he's bright. He could have been a statistic. Instead he wound up in law school on a full ride. He's a self-made man."

She didn't think Rick saw himself that way, though.

"He loves me, J.T." Anne told her brother, who chuckled.

"No kidding," he said dryly.

"God, you knew?"

"He tries pretty hard to hide it, but it's been kind of hard to miss."

Yet she had missed it. Until now.

"He's a good man."

"I've always hoped you'd figure that out," J.T. replied. Then, his tone growing serious, he added, "I've always hoped that he would, too. He's no murderer, Anne."

"Of course not. As you said, it was self-defense."

Even so, Anne knew she had to make Rick acknowledge that key distinction if they were to have a future together.

When Rick answered Anne's knock a few minutes later he was once again his reserved self. He'd shed his suit jacket and tie, though, and his shirt was untucked and still slightly wrinkled from the time it had spent on the floor of her suite. His hair was mussed, too, which Anne took as a sign that he hadn't managed to completely resurrect his dense wall of control.

"I thought we should talk," she said, worrying her hands together as she followed him inside. Her eyebrows rose when she noticed the suitcases. "Are you going somewhere?

"Tokyo office. I have some Tracker business to look into there."

"Oh, how long will you be gone?"

"Couple days. At least. If you need anything while I'm gone, I'm sure that, um, Gid, can help you."

"Gid? You want me to call Gid?"

"He's smart, efficient." He coughed and ran a hand through his hair. "Hell, the guy's damned near perfect from what I've been able to determine through background checks."

"Yes, but he's not you," she said simply.

Rick paced to the desk and shuffled some papers into file folders before stowing them in his briefcase. With his back still to Anne, he said, "I'll take a cab to the airport and leave you the rental car."

"You're just going to…go?"

"Tracker business," he said again. "It came up rather suddenly."

"I guess so. J.T. didn't mention it when we spoke on the phone a few minutes ago."

His head whipped around so quickly Anne wondered how his neck didn't snap. "You've talked to J.T.?"

She nodded. "I told him about Chisato and Izumi and how our meeting went."

"I'm sure he was happy to hear from you."

"Yes. And then I told him that I love you."

"You told him—"

"That I love you. And I mentioned that you love me, too." When his face blanched white, she added, "Don't worry. I left out the almost-sex we had on the couch in my suite. I didn't figure he'd appreciate hearing about that."

Rick's breathing grew ragged and he pulled out the chair from the desk and plunked down heavily onto its striped cushion.

"If you're feeling a little light-headed right now I can recommend the old head-between-the-knees trick."

Rick said nothing and so Anne decided to fill the silence. "You know, J.T. wasn't the least bit surprised to hear about your feelings for me. He said he'd known for a long time that you loved me."

Rick shook his head slowly, his breathing becoming even more ragged and labored when she added, "And he was genuinely pleased to hear that I'd fallen for you."

"He can't be."

"Why?"

"Because he knows—"

"That you're a good man. Self-made is how I believe he referred to you."

Rick buried his head in his hands. The words were muffled, but they still managed to pierce her heart. "I'm my father's son."

"Then you're a liar." She waited until he glanced up

before she continued. "Since the day I learned that my birth mother was still alive, you said what happened in the future was still my call. You told me I had the power to control my destiny. Well, what about you?"

"It's not the same."

"The hell it's not." She waited a beat. "Have you ever hit a woman, Rick?"

"Of course not."

"Have you ever struck a child?"

"God, no."

"And yet you're so sure you're your father's son."

"I killed him, Anne."

"You *protected* yourself. J.T. told me, Rick. He filled in all the blanks you left so damningly empty. You're no murderer. I know that. J.T. knows that. The prosecutor's office knew that when it chose not to bring charges against you more than two decades ago. When are you going to accept the truth and move on with your life?"

"I'd do it again."

"Of course you would. You're a survivor. That's nothing to be ashamed of."

He said nothing, but he looked up and she saw him swallow.

"You know, it's funny, but I didn't used to believe DNA mattered for much. Then I met Chisato and Izumi today and I felt a connection I can't quite explain. When you're adopted, you don't look at other people in your family and see, well familiarity, if that makes sense."

"You and J.T. are a lot alike."

"In temperament and we have the same voice inflections and sense of humor. Music." She shrugged. "I've given up hope for him on that score. But when I look at him, I don't see pieces of myself. I looked at Chisato and Izumi today, and I did."

"I look just like my old man," Rick replied bitterly. "I am exactly his image."

"No." Anne knelt in front of him now and gripped his hands in hers. "Is who I am dictated by the shape of my eyes or the color of my hair, Rick?"

"No, but you can't change heredity, Anne."

"Maybe you can't change it, but you can control the choices you make."

"That's what I've been doing."

"No, Rick, you've been denying yourself the right to love and be loved. Well, I do love you and I'm not going to stop. You might be able to control your emotions, but you can't control mine. How I feel, who I love, that's not up to you."

When he said nothing, Anne asked, "Whose daughter am I?"

He shook his head.

"I'm Jeanne Lundy's daughter and I'm the daughter of Chisato Nakanishi, but ultimately, neither woman is responsible for the woman I've become. I am." Anne framed his face between her hands. Wonderful bone structure, she thought again. Wonderful man. "I get to decide my future, Rick, and I'm asking you to forget your past and be a part of it. Can you do that? Will you?"

He reached up to cover her hands with his own, pressing her palms more tightly against his damp cheeks. This time, he didn't pull them away and even before he kissed her, she knew she had her answer.

EPILOGUE

"I NEED you."

No sweeter words, Rick thought, as Anne marched into his office at Tracker carrying a large package wrapped in brown paper. She was in a fine temper. Not for the first time. Not for the last. And, damn, but it looked good on her.

"Have a seat," he invited and punched the intercom to ask his assistant to hold any calls. Then, folding his hands on the desk blotter in front of him, he gave Anne his undivided attention. "You were saying something about needing me?"

"You know, smugness is not an attractive quality."

Rick raised his eyebrows and allowed a smile to lift one side of his mouth. "You thought it looked pretty good on me when I joined you in the shower this morning."

"Well, when it's the only thing you're wearing," she allowed with a sniff.

"So, what's the emergency?"

"My first show in Sapporo is less than a month off and you have to ask? I've changed my mind on one of the selections."

"Again?"

"What can I say? I need your help."

"You're not taking out the portrait of Chisato. We've gone over this half a dozen times already. It's wonderful. Inspired. She's going to love it."

"I know. It's staying in and it will hang right next to the one of my mother."

"Then what's the problem?"

"I thought I'd add this one." She handed him the package across the desk. "I wanted your opinion first, though. Open it, please."

He stood and carefully unwrapped the artwork, his breath catching as the last of the paper fell away. The Sapporo show was to be all portraits, but this wasn't a portrait. Rather, it was a collage of shots and all of them were of Rick. Some he recognized from the afternoon he and Anne had spent in a rowboat in the park. Others were shot during the months since their return to San Francisco.

She'd worked magic with her oils on each one, capturing the turbulence and desperation that had marked his life for so long, and also managing to portray the peace and healing he'd found in her love.

"Anne," he whispered, awed anew by her talent and humbled to have been her inspiration. He reached for her hand, pulled her close to his side. He didn't need to ask her to stay there. He knew that she always would. "I don't know what to say."

"Say you like it."

"I love it." He kissed her. "So, what are you calling it?"

"*Before and After.* The day I got the DNA test results

back, you told me that some events cleave our lives in two."

"I remember." He kissed her again. "And some things help mend them back together."

"That's because cleaving has more than one definition. I prefer the other one."

"The other one?"

"To hold firmly, loyally and without wavering."

"I prefer that one, too."

"I love you, Rick."

"I love you too, Mrs. Danton."

* * * * *

Louise Valentine is still smarting from the humiliation of being fired from Bella Lucia by her workaholic cousin Max, and the discovery that she was adopted as a child. Then, Max turns up on the doorstep of her successful PR and Marketing company, insisting that she do some promotions work for the family's restaurant chain. At first Louise coldly rebuffs him—but then she finds that years of secret longing for Max cannot be forgotten so easily...

Here's an exclusive extract...

"SO WHY arc you so anxious to have me come and work for you?"

Because he was crazy, he thought.

Who did he think he was kidding? Working with Louise was going to try his self-control to its limits.

He took a slow breath.

"I want you to work *with* me, Lou, not *for* me. I respect your skill, your judgment, but we both know that I could buy that out in the marketplace. What makes you special, unique, is that you've spent a lifetime breathing in the very essence of Bella Lucia. You're a Valentine to your fingertips, Louise. The fact that you're adopted doesn't alter any of that."

"It alters how I feel."

"I understand that and, for what it's worth, I think Ivy and John were wrong not to tell you the truth, but it doesn't change who or what you are. Jack wants you on board, Louise, and he's right."

"He's been chasing you? Wants to know why you haven't signed me up yet? Well, that would explain your sudden enthusiasm."

"He wanted to know the situation before he took off last week."

"Took off? Where's he gone?"

"He was planning to meet up with Maddie in Florence at the weekend. To propose to her."

"You're kidding!" And when he shook his head, "Oh, but that's so romantic!" Then, apparently recalling the way he'd flirted with Maddie at the Christmas party, she said, "Are you okay with that?"

He found her concern unexpectedly touching. "More than okay," he assured her. "I was only winding Jack up at Christmas. It's what brothers do."

"You must have really put the wind up him if he was driven to marriage," she said.

"Bearing in mind our father's poor example, I think you can be sure that he wouldn't have married her unless he loved her, Lou."

Or was he speaking for himself?

"No. Of course not. I'm sorry."

Sorry? Louise apologizing to him? That had to be a first. Things were looking up.

She laughed.

"What?"

She shook her head. "Weddings to the left of us, weddings to the right of us and not one of them held at a family restaurant." She tutted. "You know what you need, Max? Some heavyweight marketing muscle."

"I'm only interested in the best, Louise, so why don't we stop pussyfooting around, wasting time when we could be planning for the future?" The thought of an entire evening with her teasing him, drawing out concessions one by one, exacting repayment for every time he'd let her down, every humiliation, was enough to bring him out in a cold sweat. "Why don't you tell me what it's going to cost me? Your bottom line."

"You don't want to haggle?"

Definitely teasing.

"You want to see me suffer, is that it? If I call it total surrender, will that satisfy your injured pride?"

Her smile was as enigmatic as anything the Mona Lisa could offer. "Total surrender might be acceptable," she told him.

"You've got it. So, what's your price?"

"Nothing."

He stared at her, shocked out of teasing. That was it? A cold refusal?

"Nothing?" Then, when she didn't deny it, "You mean that this has all been some kind of elaborate wind-up? That you're not even going to consider my proposal?"

"As a proposal it lacked certain elements."

"Money? You know what you're worth, Louise. We're not going to quibble over a consultancy fee."

She shook her head. "No fee."

Outside the taxi the world moved on, busy, noisy. Commuters crossing en masse at the lights, the heavy diesel engine of a bus in the next lane, a distant siren. Inside it was still, silent, as if the world were holding its breath.

"No fee?" he repeated.

"I'll do what you want, Max. I'll give you—give the family—my time. It won't cost you a penny."

He didn't fall for it. Nothing came without some cost.

"You can't work without being paid, Louise."

"It's not going to be forever. I'll give you my time until…until the fourteenth. Valentine's Day. The diamond anniversary of the founding of Bella Lucia."

"Three weeks. Is that all?"

"It's all I can spare. My reward is my freedom, Max. I owe the family and I'll do this for them. Then the slate will be wiped clean."

"No…"

He didn't like the sound of that. He didn't want her for just a few weeks. Didn't want to be treated like a client, even if he was getting her time for nothing. Having fought the idea for so long, he discovered that he wanted more, a lot more from her than that.

"You're wrong. You can't just walk away, replace one family with another. You can't wipe away a lifetime of memories, of care—"

"It's the best deal you're ever likely to get," she said, cutting him short before he could add "of love…"

"Even so. I can't accept it."

"You don't have a choice," she said. "You asked for my bottom line; that's it."

"There's always a choice," he said, determined that she shouldn't back him into a corner, use Bella Lucia as a salve to her conscience, so that she could walk away without a backward glance. Something that he knew she'd come to regret.

Forget Bella Lucia.

This was more important and, if he did nothing else, he had to stop her from throwing away something so precious.

"That's my offer, Max. Take it or leave it."

"There must be something that you want, that I can offer you," he said, assailed by a gut-deep certainty that he must get her to accept something from them— from him. Make it more than a one way transaction. For her sake as much as his. "Not money," he said, quickly, "if that's the way you want it, but a token."

"A token? Anything?"

Her eyes were leaden in the subdued light of the cab, making it impossible to read what she was thinking. That had changed. There had been a time when every thought had been written across her face, as easy to read as a book.

He was going into this blind.

"Anything," he said.

"You insist?"

He nodded once.

"Then my fee for working with you on the expansion of the Bella Lucia restaurant group, Max, is…a kiss."

* * * * *

Don't miss this sizzling finale to
The Brides of Bella Lucia
Liz Fielding's
THE VALENTINE BRIDE (#3934)
out in February 2007
Find out whether Max and Louise can put their turbulent past behind them and find a future together.

In February, expect MORE
from

as it increases to six titles per month.

What's to come...

Rancher and Protector

Part of the
Western Weddings
miniseries
BY JUDY CHRISTENBERRY

The Boss's Pregnancy Proposal

BY RAYE MORGAN

Don't miss February's
incredible line up of authors!

nocturne™

WAS HE HER SAVIOR
OR HER NIGHTMARE?

HAUNTED
LISA CHILDS

Years ago, Ariel and her sisters were separated for
their own protection. Now the man who vowed
revenge on her family has resumed the hunt, and
Ariel must warn her sisters before it's too late.
The closer she comes to finding them, the more
secretive her fiancé becomes. Can she trust the man
she plans to spend eternity with? Or has he been
waiting for the perfect moment to destroy her?

On sale December 2006.

HARLEQUIN® *Romance*®

What a month!

In February watch for

Rancher and Protector

Part of the Western Weddings miniseries

BY JUDY CHRISTENBERRY

The Boss's Pregnancy Proposal

BY RAYE MORGAN

Also in February, expect
MORE of what you love
as the Harlequin Romance line
increases to six titles per month.

REQUEST YOUR FREE BOOKS!
2 FREE NOVELS PLUS 2
FREE GIFTS!

HARLEQUIN ROMANCE®

From the Heart, For the Heart

YES! Please send me 2 FREE Harlequin Romance® novels and my 2 FREE gifts. After receiving them, if I don't wish to receive any more books, I can return the shipping statement marked "cancel." If I don't cancel, I will receive 4 brand-new novels every month and be billed just $3.57 per book in the U.S., or $4.05 per book in Canada, plus 25¢ shipping and handling per book and applicable taxes, if any*. That's a savings of over 15% off the cover price! I understand that accepting the 2 free books and gifts places me under no obligation to buy anything. I can always return a shipment and cancel at any time. Even if I never buy another book from Harlequin, the two free books and gifts are mine to keep forever.

114 HDN EEV7   314 HDN EEWK

Name _____ (PLEASE PRINT)

Address _____ Apt. _____

City _____ State/Prov. _____ Zip/Postal Code _____

Signature (if under 18, a parent or guardian must sign)

Mail to the **Harlequin Reader Service®**:
IN U.S.A.: P.O. Box 1867, Buffalo, NY 14240-1867
IN CANADA: P.O. Box 609, Fort Erie, Ontario L2A 5X3

Not valid to current Harlequin Romance subscribers.

Want to try two free books from another line?
Call 1-800-873-8635 or visit www.morefreebooks.com.

* Terms and prices subject to change without notice. NY residents add applicable sales tax. Canadian residents will be charged applicable provincial taxes and GST. This offer is limited to one order per household. All orders subject to approval. Credit or debit balances in a customer's account(s) may be offset by any other outstanding balance owed by or to the customer. Please allow 4 to 6 weeks for delivery.

Your Privacy: Harlequin is committed to protecting your privacy. Our Privacy Policy is available online at www.eHarlequin.com or upon request from the Reader Service. From time to time we make our lists of customers available to reputable firms who may have a product or service of interest to you. If you would prefer we not share your name and address, please check here. ☐

HR07

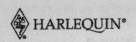
HARLEQUIN®

HARLEQUIN ROMANCE®

Coming Next Month

#3931 RANCHER AND PROTECTOR Judy Christenberry
Western Weddings
Rancher Jason Barton is all business and steely glares! Rosie Wilson has recently had a run of bad luck—but she's a fighter, and she means business, too. When they get stranded under the starlit Western sky, there's only one place Rosie wants to be: in the arms of the cowboy who has vowed to protect her.

#3932 THE VALENTINE BRIDE Liz Fielding
The Brides of Bella Lucia
Louise Valentine has been offered a job, and Max Valentine wants to help her save the family business. But since discovering she is adopted, Louise is not feeling charitable toward the Valentines. Sparks fly and soon they are both falling hard—will the past stand in the way of a special Valentine wedding?

#3933 ONE SUMMER IN ITALY... Lucy Gordon
It was supposed to be just a holiday… But then, enchanted by the pleading eyes of a motherless little girl and her brooding, enigmatic father, Matteo, Holly is swept away to their luxurious villa. Soon Holly discovers Matteo is hiding some dark secrets—her one summer in Italy is only the beginning….

#3934 THE BOSS'S PREGNANCY PROPOSAL Raye Morgan
Working for her heart-stoppingly handsome boss shouldn't have been hard for Callie, but then he asks her to have a baby with him! Of course, love wouldn't come into the arrangement—as a busy CEO, Grant wants a family, but he's been hurt before. Could sensible Callie be just what he's looking for?

#3935 CROWNED: AN ORDINARY GIRL Natasha Oakley
Just as Prince Sebastian caught a glimpse of normal life, the untimely death of his father, the King of Andovaria, forced him to leave behind his most precious gift—the love of an ordinary girl. Now, years later, Marianne Chambers is in town. Can Seb fight tradition and claim her as his very own princess?

#3936 OUTBACK BABY MIRACLE Melissa James
Heart to Heart
As untamed as the Outback land he masters, cattleman Jake Connors is a mystery to Laila. Something about him calls to her in a way no other man has. But before he can give her his heart, Jake must stop running from the demons of his past. Might Laila's pregnancy surprise be the miracle they both need?

HRCNM0107